PREMONITION

THE BOOK OF Jer3miah

PREMONITION

LUISA PERKINS and JARED ADAIR

DESERET
BOOK

Salt Lake City, Utah

Library of Congress Cataloging-in-Publication Data

Perkins, Luisa M., author.
  The book of Jer3miah : Premonition / Luisa Perkins and Jared Adair.
    pages cm
  Summary: When college freshman Jeremiah Whitney accepts the charge of a mysterious Mesoamerican box, it makes him the target of a terrifying conspiracy. As he tries to uncover the truth about the box, more questions arise and the stakes get higher.
  ISBN 978-1-60907-011-3 (paperbound)
  1. Mormon youth—Fiction. 2. Film novelizations. I. Adair, Jared, author. II. Title. III. Title: Book of Jeremiah.
  PS3616.E746B66 2012
  813'.6—dc23   2012014127

Printed in the United States of America
Edwards Brothers Malloy, Ann Arbor, MI

10 9 8 7 6 5 4 3 2 1

This book is dedicated to the memory
of the eleven students
who lost their lives in the attempt
to expose the corruption
of Gainsborough Dahl Transglobal:

David Jon Banks
Scott Clarke
John Forbyn
Phil Goodwin
Linda Johnson
Matt Love
Lyvia Martinez
Matt Pieper
Stephen Quebe
Taylor Rose
James Shores

And to Calbert Davenport
—wherever he may be—
without whom these frightening truths
would never have been brought to light.

SWIFTnet
SECURE TRANSMISSION SERVICE

To: L. Dahl, GDT, London, U.K.

From: J. Menendez, L3G1ON Central America Office, Santiago de Guayquil, Ecuador

CC: P. Gainsborough

Re: Project H3ROD Update

- - - - -

Dear Mr. Dahl:

Candidate 68, positively identified and assigned candidacy status last week in Huehuetenango, has proven difficult to observe/investigate more closely. Therefore I am doubly pleased to report that, as of this morning, our operative has procured vital records for the child. (See petty cash receipt and reimbursement request for incentive paid to the assistant town clerk following the text of this message.)

Candidate 68's date of birth is definitely outside the parameters of this cycle of the project, so we are closing his file pending your approval. However due to the suspicious nature of interactions with known 3N associates (which I realize may well be an intentional red herring), I would request that we keep the baby under a tertiary level of observation for at least the next 18 months.

As always, I await your orders with respect and dedication.

DATE: 07 MAY 2002   EVIDENCE FILE #: 1.19.19.11

DESC.: FROM THE JOURNAL OF JEREMIAH WHITNEY

Today I killed Rusty, and now we have to move.

Mom left yesterday to go take care of Grandma Price in Manti. She called late last night when she got off the plane. I guess it's a long way from Baltimore to Utah.

I miss Mom already, especially now that my poor dog is dead. But Grandma is having surgery, and she needs Mom's help, so Dad and I are on our own this week. Dad said we could go to the batting cages and order pizza and have a <u>Star Wars</u> marathon while Mom was gone, but now we can't—not after what happened today.

Last night, Dad bought some cold cereal for me to eat this week. Since Mom always makes hot breakfast, this was my junk food treat. Dad says it's our tradition. He got my two favorite kinds—Power Flakes and Krispy Kritters. Krispy Kritters is the best, and this box had a special offer to send away for a free BinFreak video game preview.

But when I took the cereal box out of the cupboard this morning, I got a bad feeling about it. It was like the box had this dark halo all around it, and it smelled really nasty. But it wasn't a real smell. It doesn't make sense, but I could <u>feel</u>, somewhere behind my nose, that the cereal was bad even though it looked normal. I put the box down and got out the Power Flakes, but they had that same <u>rotten</u> feeling.

Rusty was jumping around like he always does in the morning. I opened the door to let him out back so he could do his business. He wouldn't go out, though. He just stared at me and whined. Then he wagged his tail some more. With his

2

tongue hanging out, he always makes me laugh, because it looks like he's smiling.

Dad came in all stressed like he usually is in the mornings and told me to pour a bowl of cereal for him, too. He said he'd eat his after he got out of the shower. I tried to tell him that the cereal was poison or something.

He checked the box, but it was sealed up, and the expiration date was next January, so he told me it was fine. He said that was all there was for breakfast and that I'd have to wait until lunch at school if I didn't eat that cereal, because there wasn't really anything else to eat in the house, and he couldn't be late for work today.

I tried not to argue, but there was no way I could eat that cereal. He got a little mad at me, like he does sometimes when he thinks I'm being picky and stubborn about stuff. I'm not picky, but I guess I am stubborn. I didn't want to cause a problem, not again. So I poured two bowls of Krispy Kritters and put them on the kitchen table—just so he would go take his shower. He gave me a look, but he left when I got the milk out of the fridge.

Except, when I heard the shower going, I put the milk back and looked at the cereal boxes again. The danger I was sensing was still there, stronger than ever. This was definitely life or death. I knelt down on the kitchen floor and prayed. I asked God to help me, because I knew that Dad and I could NOT eat those Krispy Kritters. NO WAY. Help Dad see that I'm not being a weirdo, I asked. Help him see that there's something really wrong here.

While I was still on the cold tile with my eyes closed, I heard Rusty jump up on the table. I said Amen fast and got up and ran over there, but it was too late. Rusty eats

3

faster than any dog in the world, and most of the cereal was in his gut in just a few seconds.

Rusty, NO! I yelled, and he jumped off the table and came over to me, wagging his tail so hard that his whole backside wiggled. He knows I can't get mad at him. But I wasn't mad. I was scared. He put his front paws on my shoulders like he's not supposed to, but I didn't tell him to get down. I just hugged him and let him lick my face. Maybe the cereal was only poisonous to humans—I hoped.

But then it happened. Rusty kind of collapsed and knocked me over, too. I fell hard on my bum, and my elbow smacked the tile. But Rusty was way worse off. He coughed this awful, deep cough, and white foam started coming out of his mouth and dripping on the floor. His legs scrabbled on the tile, and his whole body twitched like he was getting electric shocks. He yawned really wide and his eyeballs went all white, and then he lay still.

I screamed and cried. The best dog in the whole world was dead, and it was my fault.

Dad came in dripping wet with a towel on. What is it? he yelled, but then he came around the kitchen island and saw Rusty and me on the floor. He looked at us, and he looked at the table with the mostly empty cereal bowls and fell to his knees beside me. He said a super bad word that I didn't even know he knew. And he grabbed me and hugged me hard.

What happened to your face? he asked.

I said I didn't know, but suddenly I realized that my right cheek was itching really bad and my eye felt puffy and like I couldn't open it all the way. That's where Rusty was licking me, I said. I looked down at my fingers, and they were big and red like hot dogs. I had used them to open the cereal box. I cried even harder because maybe you didn't have to eat the poison, you only had to touch it.

Dad hugged me again and got up and ran to get some Benadryl and made me take it, even though it makes me super sleepy. I can't go to school on Benadryl, I said. I have a test in Social Studies today.

You're not going to school, Dad said. We have to pack. We have to leave. Today. But first go take a shower and scrub everywhere Rusty touched you. And throw away those clothes.

That was bad luck because that shirt was one of my favorites. But I knew Dad was right. In my heart, I knew. And I was glad that he knew now, too.

Dad got dressed and put on gloves and hauled Rusty out in the backyard and buried him. Then Dad came in the house and put the cereal boxes in two big black garbage bags and threw them away outside. After that, he wiped down the table and mopped the floor with bleach. Then he threw away the gloves, washed his hands for a super long time, and took some Benadryl, too.

When it wasn't so early in Utah, he called Mom and told her what had happened. He went into his room and shut the door halfway through their conversation, but I sat by the air vent so I could hear what he said.

It was a lot of stuff I didn't understand—something called GDT and how it was casting a wide net and that he and Mom knew that this day would come. It had come before, just not as dramatically, he told her. It was always just a matter of time before they closed in on us.

Who? Who is tracking us down? And why do they want me dead? What kind of monster would put poison in a kid's cereal? And how did Dad get just the right box at the

5

store? Were they all poisoned, or did someone sneak into our house and poison them while we were sleeping last night?

These questions scared me so bad that I couldn't really even think about them, because every time I did, it's like I got paralyzed.

I can't believe we have to move AGAIN. I can't believe we have to leave Rusty all alone here. I was just getting used to Baltimore. I looked Toronto up in the road atlas when Dad told me that's where we are moving now. I've never been to Canada before.

Dad, what about your job? I asked. What about our _Star Wars_ marathon? I knew I was being a baby, but Rusty dying like that had me freaked out and I missed Mom like crazy.

We'll have our marathon when we get to Canada, he promised me. Then he told me to get some empty boxes out of the basement and start packing up my books and stuff. Mom will meet us there, so you and I will just have to do our best with this move, he said.

So I'm in my room, and I'm supposed to be working fast. But I had a feeling J should write all this down before we left.

This is all my fault. Poor, poor Rusty. I know God answered my prayer about showing Dad the danger, but did it have to be in such an awful way? I don't know if I would have prayed if I knew Rusty was going to be the sacrifice. He was my only friend in the world, and I killed him. And he didn't even have a funeral. I already miss him so bad. I know he is in dog heaven and that I will see him again one day. I hope when I do, he will forgive me for killing him. My whole chest hurts like my heart is really broken. If families are forever, does that mean that pets are, too?

CHAPTER ONE

A Sacred Trust:
December 2008

"No way. Are you serious?"

Jeremiah gasped as he tore away the wrapping paper that enveloped his present. His momentary embarrassment over opening a birthday gift in the parking lot of his college dorm vanished. His parents had gone over the top and gotten him a video camera—only the smallest, hottest, best one on the market. He felt bad because he knew his parents couldn't afford this—not on top of his college expenses—but he couldn't stop smiling.

The lens cap dangled from the front of the camera on a tiny cord. Jeremiah turned the camera around in his hands and looked through the viewfinder. He laughed. No wonder his parents couldn't wait until they got to Manti to have him open this. Now he really wished they didn't have to go to the family reunion; he wanted to stay here and film everything.

"Happy birthday, honey." His mother hugged him from the side. Still looking through the camera, Jeremiah turned to face her. She waved him away.

He caught sight of a pretty coed walking toward her car.

When she saw him filming her, she smiled and gave a seductive wave, mugging for his benefit.

"Jeremiah! Don't be creepy," his mom said.

He felt his face go hot as he turned the camera away from the girl. He had been at college for four months, but already he had learned that college girls—at least, the ones that went to school here—were a lot more forward than any he had known in high school. These women would ask you out in the most businesslike of ways, as if you were a car they wanted to test drive. It had struck him as a little weird. Of course, girls might think he was the weird one if he kept randomly filming them—even if it was with the coolest camera of all time.

Jeremiah turned around in the parking lot, surveying his surroundings through the lens of his new toy. He pushed a button, and everything went green. So cool. "It's got night vision!"

"Only the best," Debra said.

"Slow motion . . ." Jeremiah toggled another switch and zoomed in on the mountains. The detail was incredible. He could see branches on the pines below the tree line on Mount Timpanogos. He gazed at the mountains for a few seconds then swished around to face his parents again. As he did so, a man in the parking lot ducked out of view. Seriously? What a crank. It's not like Jeremiah was from a news network, or something. The guy didn't look like a paparazzi-avoiding celebrity. What did he care if he got caught on video?

"I hope it wasn't too much," Jeremiah said to his dad.

He squinted at the little red, flashing monitor that was tucked under the eyepiece. "Hey . . . it's recording?"

His dad laughed. "We wanted to save your reaction for your posterity. You know how you love your journal. We thought this would be another way you could record your life."

Jeremiah turned and filmed his mother again. She covered her face with her hands.

"Okay, turn it off—at least off me!"

Instead of obeying, Jeremiah zoomed in on her face— the kindest eyes and readiest smile he had ever known. His mom was the best. So was his dad. Roger and Debra Whitney: Parents of the Year. He knew she was happy right now, and he wanted to do exactly what his dad had just said—preserve the moment.

"No, smile," he said. "This is for your posterity."

She rolled her eyes and sighed. "At least let me fix my hair."

Jeremiah's dad kidded her. "You should have thought of that when you handed it to him, sweetheart."

Jeremiah turned and pointed the camera up at the dorm's second story. His roommate was going to go nuts over this. "Hey, can we go show Porter?"

"Ah, the infamous Porter. All right. We should probably meet him in person anyway, just to put a little fear into him. But five minutes, okay? We're already late, and Aunt Marilyn hates that."

Jeremiah's dad started for the dorm, then turned back. "Oh, and Miah—grab the box in case you need to return it."

"I won't need to return it, but—" he definitely wanted the instruction manual. He planned to take full advantage of every feature. His mind already swam with the possibilities of what he could film. This was the best present he'd ever gotten.

He opened the door of his parents' minivan and grabbed the box.

"Lock the door," his father called. Whatever. The van didn't have anything that any normal college student would take, but Jeremiah knew how paranoid his dad could get. It didn't make sense to irritate him at his point. He pushed the little lock stick down and shut the door.

"Did you lock it?" his mom asked. "Come on, then." Jeremiah loped up the sidewalk and caught up with them. He was about to switch off the camera, but then stopped.

An overwhelming feeling hit him—he needed to keep filming. *What?* That made no sense. But he had learned long ago not to ignore this kind of prompting. It wasn't anxiety—it was a calm, but very direct sort of voice within him that had always kept him safe in the past, as long as he paid attention to it. The very few times he hadn't, he had regretted it.

His mom turned around again. "Miah! Turn it off. You'll burn out the batteries or something."

"No, you can recharge the batteries." Jeremiah kept his voice light. Most of the time, his parents supported him whenever he followed a prompting, but sometimes—when they were stressed or preoccupied—they got frustrated and annoyed. And those seemed to be the times that it was most crucial that he pay attention and obey.

He didn't want any friction on his birthday—especially since there was bound to be some between his father and Aunt Marilyn once they got to the family reunion—but he had to listen to the voice.

Sure enough, his dad was in a single-minded, "go-to" mode. "Shut it off, son. We're in a hurry. You'll break your neck going up those stairs if your focus is glued to that thing."

Jeremiah's feeling grew stronger. Filming what they were doing was important. No way could he shut off the camera, not now. Why didn't his dad get it after all these years? Why didn't he recognize that Jeremiah wasn't just following a whim? But he tried to keep things casual. "What's the big deal? I just want to film this."

"Jeremiah." His mom's eyes pled. His dad was getting worked up, and she, too, wanted to avoid any conflict.

"I *need* to film this," he said simply, praying they'd understand.

"Not another one of your 'feelings,'" said his dad through gritted teeth. He took a deep breath and visibly relaxed. "Listen," he continued in a calmer voice, "I know the Holy Ghost tells you lots of things, but He doesn't tell you to film people walking into buildings. That makes no sense. This is just an ordinary day—except for the fact that it's your birthday, of course." He forced a smile, and Jeremiah's mother shot her husband one of her looks. He volleyed one right back, not backing down.

Jeremiah decided to try to make peace. "Fine," he said, ostentatiously flipping the "off" switch. As soon as his dad opened the dorm's door, Jeremiah surreptitiously switched the camera on again.

"Off!" his dad tossed over his shoulder, and Jeremiah complied. For about fifteen seconds, anyway.

On the landing, Jeremiah could hear his dad puffing a bit. "Just one more flight of stairs," he assured his parents.

"It hasn't changed since I was here," his dad said, looking around at the walls of the stairwell.

His wife elbowed him. "In 1922?"

"Hey—" And just like that, Dad's good humor was restored. Jeremiah's mom had a special kind of magic. Maybe it was just because his parents had been married for twenty years, but his mom knew exactly how to diffuse his dad's tension every time. Jeremiah wondered for the thousandth time whether he would ever find anyone who understood him as well as his parents understood one another.

He held the camera low so that his dad wouldn't see that it was on again. He pointed with his other hand down the hallway as they got to his floor. "Over this way, we have a game room . . . we've got vending machines . . ."

He stopped, engulfed in a giant bear hug—and then he felt the bear reaching for his new present. Porter. "Whoa, you're gonna break it!" He tried to maneuver out of his roommate's grasp, but Porter was just too big.

"Hey!" his dad said, deftly snatching the camera from Jeremiah's grasp.

Porter let go of him and pulled down his tank top, which

had ridden up to expose his flabby belly. Jeremiah tried not to laugh. Lilah must not have reminded Porter to wash his clothes this week. His overflowing laundry bag lay at his feet, and he had clearly run out of underwear—again. A few weeks earlier, Porter had used one of those home dry cleaning kits on a pair of underwear before church—but he must have run out of such emergency measures.

Porter grinned at Jeremiah. "Is that a new camera, birthday boy? Way cool. Hey, we should hide it in Brian's room. Maybe we can uncover a conspiracy." He looked at Jeremiah's guests, then shook his hair out of his eyes and straightened his spine a bit. "So, you must be Mom and Dad." Jeremiah's dad nodded, while his mom tried to look anywhere but at Porter's state of undress. Porter stuck out his hand. "I'm Porter, your son's babysitter—"

"Roommate," Jeremiah interrupted, taking the bait even though he knew Porter was just trying to get a rise out of him. That's just how Porter showed his affection—by merciless teasing. Porter continued as if Jeremiah hadn't spoken.

"—which is a full-time job, you know, with all the ladies—"

Jeremiah elbowed his roommate in the ample gut.

His mom blanched. "Ladies?"

Porter guffawed. "Joking! Your son's like a monk, actually." He glanced at Jeremiah. "You know, you should really date a little more. You're only a freshman once."

Jeremiah couldn't resist the impulse to needle Porter back a little bit. "Or twice, in your case." He looked at his mom, willing her not to take Porter so seriously. He knew his roommate looked like a hapless slob, but Jeremiah had discovered pure gold underneath, and he loved the guy like the older brother he'd never had. "This is Porter's second try. He got kicked out his first time, but that was before his mission."

His mom stuck her chin out a little; Jeremiah could tell she was trying to assert her motherliness. "Yes, well, speaking of which, now's the time for you to focus on studying and missionary preparation."

"Dating isn't against the commandments," Jeremiah's dad said with a grimace.

Porter laughed again. "O-ho! Chalk one up for Dad." He narrowed his eyes at Jeremiah's father and made a face as if in deep thought. "So, are you gonna take us out for dinner tonight?"

"No," Jeremiah answered before his dad could say something rude. "We have a family reunion in Manti. Here." He handed the camera box to his roommate. "Can you just take this to our room?"

Porter never missed an opportunity to negotiate. "Can I use your meal ticket?"

Jeremiah smiled. He pulled his meal card out of his pocket and handed it over. Porter winked and bent to pick up his overflowing laundry bag.

"We're late," Jeremiah's dad said. "Nice meeting you, Porter."

Porter ducked his head and started down the stairs.

"Porter!" Jeremiah's mother called down the stairwell after him. He stopped on the landing and looked back up.

"He's my only son," she said, and it sounded to Jeremiah like her voice was rough with unshed tears; he wondered why she was getting all emotional all of a sudden. "So keep him on the straight and narrow, huh?"

Porter grinned again and nodded. Jeremiah recognized that his roommate's manners were the worst, but there was no denying his charm. His mother's shoulders relaxed. "See ya, Mom and Dad," Porter called, and bounded down the stairs.

Debra leaned over the railing. "And, Porter! Put on a shirt!" After a pause, she added, "Son."

She turned back to Jeremiah. "I thought he was a returned missionary," she said, her eyes wide with bewilderment—but fortunately keeping her voice down.

"Oh, he is," Jeremiah assured her. How had Porter characterized his attitude toward the gospel? Oh, right. Jeremiah chuckled. "He says he holds onto the iron rod with a bungee cord."

His mother frowned at this—he'd meant it as a joke, but she could never joke about "kids today" going astray.

"Don't tell me that. I just hope you act more mature after your mission."

I already do, Jeremiah protested in his mind, but said nothing.

"*I* just hope you don't live in the dorms after your mission," Roger said, obviously trying to lighten the mood. That was his parents—always concerned for each other, always trying to make one another happy.

"Can I have the camera back?" Jeremiah asked. His

dad handed it to him, seeming not to have noticed that it had been on all this time. Jeremiah followed his parents as they hurried down the stairs. It was probably good that they hadn't made it all the way to Jeremiah's dorm room. What would his parents say about Porter's mammoth recliner that took up half of their living space—or the swear-peppered quotes from his notorious ancestor, Porter Rockwell, that Porter had scrawled on notepaper and duct-taped to the walls? Jeremiah's laughter echoed in the stairwell.

Once they were outside, Jeremiah ran around them, then backed toward the parking lot while keeping the camera aimed at them.

"You're going to run into a car if you keep walking backward like that," his mom said. She stopped when they got to the van, frowning as she looked through the passenger window. She jiggled the door handle. It was still locked.

"Honey? Did you put something in here?"

"No." When would any of them have had time to do that? They had been together since they left the car.

"It has Jeremiah's name on it."

Jeremiah leaned the camera in so that he could see his mother's seat. On it sat a cream-colored envelope, big and square. It looked like a wedding invitation or a graduation announcement, or something fancy like that.

"It wasn't there when we left. I locked the car," Jeremiah said.

Were his parents kidding around again? Maybe it was another birthday card. Did they have another surprise for him? Jeremiah hoped not. You didn't turn eighteen every day, but they'd already spent way too much on him. He knew his mom was thinking about taking a part-time job to ease the strain on their finances.

Roger unlocked the car and retrieved the envelope. He looked at Jeremiah, who nodded. "Open it."

Inside was a card that looked like it was made out of some kind of really old paper. A funny symbol was stamped on it—a stylized sun with three rectangles in its center. Roger turned it over. In old-fashioned typescript it read, "Manti Library—go immediately."

Jeremiah looked at his father, who had glanced at his mother with fear and regret in his eyes. Something passed between his parents; Jeremiah hated how they could communicate with a single look while leaving him out of the conversation. He looked back at the card.

"Who knew we were going to Manti?" he wondered aloud, and zoomed in on the words on the card with his camera.

"Shut it off," his father said—and this time, Jeremiah obeyed.

He climbed into the car. "Hey, does anyone want to fill me in on what's going on?" But he knew that whatever it was, his parents weren't ready to tell him. Not yet, anyway. Jeremiah closed his eyes in frustration. He was eighteen now. It was about time he got treated like an adult.

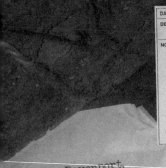

DATE: ACQUIRED 13 OCTOBER 2008   EVIDENCE FILE #: 3.2.9.9

DESC.: THREATENING LETTER

NOTES: EVIDENCE FILED WITH A COMPLAINT TO THE FRANKLIN COUNTY SHERIFF'S
OFFICE BY CYNTHIA DAVENPORT, 3295 SOUTH RIVIERA, ROCKY MOUNTAIN, VA.
EVIDENCE REGISTRY NOTES THAT THE COMPLAINANT REPORTED THAT THIS LETTER
WAS WRAPPED AROUND A BRICK AND THROWN THROUGH HER KITCHEN WINDOW
TWO NIGHTS PREVIOUS.
NO SIGNATURE OR FINGERPRINTS.
LETTER WAS PRINTED ON GENERIC WATERMARKED PAPER AVAILABLE
AT ANY OFFICE SUPERSTORE USING AN INKJET PRINTER, ALSO OF
INDETERMINATE PROVENANCE.

Dear Mrs. Davenport,

We hope this note finds you and your daughters Katie and Kelly healthy and safe.

We thought someone should make you aware of the dangerous and frankly libelous nature of the work your estranged husband is doing at the university. Though we are fully aware that you and the professor are separated at the moment, we suggest you use your strongest methods of persuasion to get him to leave off the line of inquiry he is pursuing at the present time.

We hate to involve you, an innocent bystander, in the resolution of this issue, but our office has sent several cease and desist letters to your husband's work address, all of which seem to have been ignored.

We can tell that the professor is a man who loves his family. We know this because, despite your legal separation, he attended Katie's piano recital and Kelly's dance competition with you recently. He certainly seems to be an attentive father when the four of you play tennis at the YMCA or spend family nights at the Holiday Bowl over in Boone's Mill. We applaud your efforts to maintain a semblance of family togetherness for the sake of your children despite your differences as a couple. A family man as diligent and concerned at home as Calbert Davenport is will surely see reason when the mother of his children explains it to him.

We are confident that we will not have to resort to contacting Kelly at Benjamin Franklin Middle School or Katie at Waid Elementary School to ask for their aid in this matter. While we know well the effectiveness of the tearful pleas of daughters to their fathers—especially long distance—we ask you to assure us that such measures will not be necessary in this instance.

If you tell Calbert to destroy his research into GDT and its affiliates, we are confident that you and your family will remain intact and happy in this beautiful part of the country.

Ancient and Modern

███████████:

Exposing Utah's ███████ ██████

DR. CALBERT DAVENPORT
Comparative Symbologist

08 DECEMBER 2008

FLYER FOR CANCELLED COLLEGE LECTURE & PHOTO OF C. DAVENPORT

EVIDENCE FILE #: 3.9.37.25

WIDELY DISTRIBUTED FLYER FOR LECTURE ABOUT CONSPIRACIES, WITH DATE, TIME AND URL REDACTED BY UNKNOWN INDIVIDUAL(S)

PHOTO (OR VIDEO STILL) OF DR. CALBERT DAVENPORT, SCHEDULED LECTURER FOR EVENT; VIDEO SOURCE UNKNOWN

A lecture by

DR. CALBERT H. DAVENPORT

CHAPTER TWO

The Library

Elizabethan Report's great new hit single was playing on the car radio as they drove down I-15, but Jeremiah was too distracted to ask his mom to turn up the volume. He usually enjoyed gazing out at the mountains and the austere landscape on the way to Manti, but all he could think about now was the mysterious card he held. The paper felt like it was expensive—handmade and heavy—its fine surface catching on his callused fingers. The writing looked like it had been produced by a master calligrapher. What in the world could it possibly mean?

As he stared at it, a familiar feeling welled within him, starting somewhere around his stomach and growing until it filled his chest—the same kind of thing he had felt in the dorm parking lot just minutes ago. A warning—different from anxiety or nervousness or fear—a calm, but stern warning. What was its focus? The "invitation" to go to the Manti Library?

Yes. That was it, he knew it. He had to go there now.

He ran his mind over some of the other times he had

felt this way. A black-coated stranger watching him from beyond the schoolyard's chain-link fence in third grade. A faulty carnival ride at the county fair a year later. A shifty-eyed "salesman" at the front door. Each one had stood out suddenly to Jeremiah—outlined in shadow, with a pulsing, sickly light only he could see, urging him to get away quickly.

"I really feel like we need to stop at the library before the reunion."

Roger sighed with exasperation. "We don't have time for another one of your *feelings,* okay?"

Why was his dad being so dense? It was like he was spiritually blocked, somehow. *Warning* pulsed within Jeremiah's mind and heart. He couldn't ignore it; he couldn't deny it.

Then it hit him like a lightning bolt, and he cried out, "Dad, pull over right *now.*"

With a deafening blast on its air horn, a huge semi swerved into the right lane, nearly crashing into the minivan as it fishtailed on the wet highway. His dad jerked the steering wheel to the right and braked hard on the road's shoulder, Jeremiah's mother screaming an accompaniment the entire time.

The truck shot away from them, and she reached over and leaned on the horn. "Get off the road, you dingbat! We could've been killed!"

Despite his fear, Jeremiah smiled at the absurdity of what she'd said. "Dingbat" was as close to profanity as his mother ever trod. "I told you to pull over," he muttered, mostly to himself. He was too relieved to be bitter that his father had once again ignored him.

His dad knew he was wrong, Jeremiah could tell, because he worked hard to minimize the situation and deflect the blame. "Give the guy a break," he said, laying a calming hand on his wife's arm. "Those things have huge blind spots."

She would have none of it, moving into full righteous indignation. "Did you see that? He didn't even have any license plates! The nerve! He probably picked up some floozy from the truck stop . . ."

Though Jeremiah was sitting in back, he knew his father was now rolling his eyes. They had been through this routine before. "Not the floozy thing. . . ."

They sat in silence on the side of the highway for a few more minutes. Jeremiah looked out at the desolate, snowy fields and the monotonous grey sky to the west and felt his heartbeat slow. He assumed his dad was giving himself a moment for the same reason—to get out of panic mode. Finally, his dad pulled back onto the road and moved forward once more. The warning's urgency had subsided, but he still felt troubled on a low, disquieting level. The danger wasn't over yet.

They had reached the outskirts of Manti, farms giving way to older houses in more tightly organized neighborhoods. The temple sat on a high hill to the east, serenely presiding over the small desert city. Jeremiah had always loved the legends about Manti—that Moroni had traveled here on his way to Cumorah and dedicated the exact ground on which the temple now stood. Jeremiah could imagine Nephites and Lamanites battling nearby, and he wondered whether one of Manti's fabled caves had ever been one of Moroni's hideouts.

They made their way into town. Bare trees marched down both sides of the road in strict ranks, planted long ago by property owners with exacting standards. Jeremiah noticed a white-haired man moving snow, gripping his shovel with bright yellow work gloves. It was bitter cold out, but the man moved with energy and grace. People out here in the boonies were tough. His grandparents were that way. They just got stuff done, no matter the hardship—but they were always ready to help someone in need, too. For the first time, he looked forward to arriving at the family reunion and seeing his extended family.

The old man looked up at the minivan as it passed, his blue eyes seeming to lock onto Jeremiah's. Even though Jeremiah was behind tinted windows, he quickly looked away from the man, embarrassed to have been caught staring.

Glancing across the street, he saw a large, pale green, art deco building that looked out of place looming over the tidy russet brick houses surrounding it. He felt a little turned around; he didn't remember coming into town this way in all the times he'd visited Manti. Maybe his dad had taken a different route on purpose. He must have. His dad had grown up here and knew this place better than anyone.

Jeremiah took it as a sign. "Hey, look! There's the library."

His dad pulled up to the curb, probably trying to make up for not having listened to Jeremiah minutes before. He gazed at the library and then glanced at the car's digital clock. "It's after five. They're closed. We'll come back tomorrow, I promise." He put the car back in drive and started rolling again.

What? Was this a drive-by, just so his dad could say he'd tried? *Not good enough, Dad.*

Jeremiah opened the minivan's sliding door and jumped out. His father screeched to a halt again.

"Jeremiah," his mother yelled out the window. "Don't be unreasonable!"

Jeremiah ignored her and took the wide concrete steps to the library's double doors two at a time.

"Get back in the car! We're late!"

But Jeremiah could hear resignation in his father's voice. He tried to open the library's glass front door, but it was locked. That made no sense. They'd left Provo right after finding the mysterious invitation. Why would he be told to come here "immediately" if no one was around to greet him when he got here? Maybe he should go around back to see whether there was another entrance. He turned, catching his father's relieved smile at the fact that he couldn't get into the building.

But then several loud clicks came from behind Jeremiah, and he wheeled around to see a tall, severely dressed woman staring at him cautiously from the now half-open door. "Jeremiah? Let me see the card."

He'd forgotten he was holding it. He handed it to her.

She examined the strange symbol on it closely, then looked up and down the street.

In a clear, but low voice, she called, "Roger, Debra. Go to the next block, turn left, and come through the alley to the back door." She turned back to Jeremiah. "Quickly. Let me have your camera."

Somehow, Jeremiah knew he could trust her. Despite her formal appearance and solemn manner, she radiated a kind of warmth—though she also seemed quite nervous. He gave the camera to her, and she inspected it carefully. Nodding, she beckoned him in and double-locked the door after he stepped inside. He followed her without a word through the dark, echoing hallways to a door in the back of the building. The woman checked the rear parking lot, let Jeremiah's parents in, then locked this door as well. Jeremiah and his parents hurried to keep up as she moved to a dark staircase and started downward.

At the bottom of the stairs, the woman turned to Jeremiah's father. "You need to film this," she directed, handing him the camera. He obediently fumbled with the controls in the half light. His parents were being so docile; this wasn't like them. They must have a clue as to what all this meant. Why wouldn't they let him in on the secret? As of today, he was an adult, right?

"What's going on?" he asked. His voice echoed. This room must be much larger than it had looked at first glance. His dad moved the camera up and down to catch the view of long, high banks of small, wooden lockers. What was this room? Some sort of secure archive? What would anyone in sleepy old Manti need with this many secret hiding places? His mother took Jeremiah's arm and held it tightly. Jeremiah looked down at her shadowed face. Did she know why they were here? He got the sense that she was bracing herself for something unpleasant, but she kept silent. Jeremiah shivered with unease.

The woman stopped, pushed over a rolling staircase from one corner, and placed it in front of a column of the stacked lockers. She climbed up to the top cabinet, took its lock in her hand, and spun its combination quickly. She opened the locker's wooden door, revealing another, much more high tech combination lock.

"What is your birth date?" she asked Jeremiah.

"It's today. December 7th, 1990."

The woman punched the digits into the keypad and pulled on the door. Nothing. The woman scowled down at his mother.

"What's his *real* birthday?" Her tone said she wasn't used to people messing around with her.

His mother looked at Jeremiah, pleading in her expression. Then she sighed and closed her eyes. "April 11th, 1990."

"What?" asked Jeremiah.

Shock pulsed through him. His mom had to be kidding. Was this some sort of elaborate birthday prank? Jeremiah wouldn't put that past his father, actually. Sometimes he had a bizarre sense of humor.

But when the woman entered the second set of numbers,

the light on the digital keypad turned green. He was eight months older than he'd thought all his life? What was going on here? Furious, he looked at both of his parents. Neither of them would meet his eyes.

The locker opened with a hiss. The woman reached inside and took a wooden box from within. The box was perfectly cubical, but its dark wood looked scarred and weathered with age. As the woman descended the stairs with it cradled in her arms, Jeremiah could see that the simple design etched on the box's top was the same as the one on the mysterious card they had found in the minivan—a stylized sun with uneven rays and three parallel rectangles in its center. Was that some kind of logo? What did it mean? Metal hinges and clasps that looked handmade held the box's lid closed, and some sort of substance was smeared all the way around its edge—sealing wax?

The woman looked into Jeremiah's eyes, her face as impassive as a statue's. "This box is a sacred trust. There are three rules you must obey with exactness. The first: the box must remain in your possession at all times, or it must be concealed in a secure location."

The box was pretty bulky; Jeremiah couldn't feature carrying it around in his backpack all the time. Was there any place in his dorm room that could be considered a "secure location?" But the woman didn't pause at all for questions.

"The second: unless prompted to do so, you must not tell anyone about this box—no matter the threat—and there will be many."

Threats? What kind of threats? This wasn't something illegal, was it? What was in the thing, anyway?

"Third: do not open it until directed."

She inhaled slowly as if gathering herself. "I cannot impress upon you enough the seriousness of this trust. Do you understand?"

His father broke in, his voice harsh with distrust. "What kind of threats?"

The woman didn't answer. Jeremiah glanced at his father. There was something going on here. His dad knew something about this box, and he didn't like that this was happening right now. Jeremiah looked at his mother. Fear and love warred in her eyes. This was upsetting his parents, and he had had enough drama for one day. It was his birthday, for Pete's sake!

Except, apparently, it wasn't. Anger flared within him. He stuck out his chin and raised his eyes to the woman's once more. "I don't want it," he said flatly.

The woman looked taken aback; it appeared she hadn't expected this reaction. She looked at Jeremiah's parents for help.

His dad was on his side, for once in his life. "You can't force him to take it."

"Roger," said Jeremiah's mother in her classic *be reasonable* tone. Jeremiah sensed that he *had* to take the box, and that his mom was reminding her husband of it. They shared another one of their looks.

The woman kept her eyes fixed on Jeremiah, as if

demanding that he return his attention to her. She nodded reluctantly. "This is your choice, Jeremiah."

Jeremiah felt like he should accept the box and the instructions he had been given, but he had no desire at all to follow this particular prompting.

"I can't. I really can't." Couldn't they be done with this now? This place felt like something out of a horror movie. The shadows all around them seemed to gather and deepen. Jeremiah was creeped out, and more than a little hungry. He suddenly craved the comfortable boredom, normalcy—and delicious ham and funeral potatoes—of Aunt Marilyn's dining room table.

Crash. Something moved from deep within the bowels of the library's basement. Smaller booms and bangs followed, and the banks of fluorescent lights rattled high above them. A little dust sifted down. With a look of panic, the woman hurriedly returned the box to its locker. Jeremiah suddenly felt like he was trapped in a dungeon. There were other people down here? They certainly didn't sound friendly.

His mother squeezed his arm. "Jeremiah. You've always known what it was you needed to do."

She was right. She usually was, and she knew her son better than anyone did. His mother had been the one who had taught him to listen within himself and follow the Spirit he felt in his heart. He had witnessed her do it herself many times, which meant much more to him than any words she might have ever said.

Jeremiah searched inside for his sense of discernment,

which always fled in the face of frustration or anger. He deliberately quieted his mind and urged himself toward peace, even as the mysterious rattling and crashes intensified around him.

"We need to leave," said the woman.

His father reached over and grasped Jeremiah's shoulder. His irritation had vanished, and he looked at his son with love and concern. "You *know*, son."

"Listen," his mother whispered.

Jeremiah closed his eyes. *There.* A pinpoint of light rose within his heart. It grew as he gave it his full attention, shutting out the world around him. Within the light, he saw the box and saw the rightness of himself holding it.

Yes. Taking the box was the correct thing to do. He swallowed hard and nodded, accepting the compulsion he felt. He opened his eyes and stepped forward.

"Give me the box." His voice rang out with authority in the dark passageway.

The woman swiftly punched the numbers on the combination lock, swung the locker door open, and handed the box to Jeremiah. It was much heavier than he expected it to be. He examined the designs on it, which were more intricate than they had appeared at first. He looked at his parents, one at a time, for support, then back at the woman. "So, when should I open it?"

The woman shook her head. "I don't know. That's all I've been told."

Another crash resounded through the dim basement, much closer this time.

"Quickly, now," the woman said, as she descended the ladder. She ran down the length of the passage and stopped at the intersecting pathway. An empty garbage can stood at the junction. The woman grabbed the black plastic liner out of it and handed it to Jeremiah. "Put the box in here," she said with great intensity. "No one must see it."

Jeremiah obeyed as they walked swiftly to the staircase. His parents kept looking around nervously, as if they expected to be attacked at any moment.

"Turn off the camera," the woman directed, and they hurried up the steps to the back door.

She let them out the back way, exiting the library herself, and locking the door behind her. "Go—now," she said, and ran down the alley without a backward glance. Despite her high heels and the icy asphalt, she ran quickly and with athletic grace.

"Let's go," ordered Jeremiah's father, running to the car door. "I want to be well away from here before whoever was down there finds us and sees which direction we're headed."

His mother followed. Jeremiah glanced back at the library door. How had anyone known where they would be? It couldn't be coincidence that someone else had been in the library basement after closing time. The sense of danger grew within Jeremiah as he got in the car. His father revved the engine and peeled out of the parking lot, skidding slightly on the slick pavement.

Jeremiah sat in the back seat and stared down at the plastic bag on his lap. What on earth had he gotten himself into by taking this thing? His parents clearly knew something about what was going on, and Jeremiah found himself wishing that this all might be some carefully orchestrated joke his father was playing.

For Jeremiah's twelfth birthday, his dad had gotten an exploding piñata. That had *not* ended well. Fortunately, none of the party guests had gotten hurt, but his dad had spent several hours in the emergency room, getting treated for second-degree burns on his arm.

The box, though—it was no prank. Jeremiah couldn't ignore the feelings of confirmation he'd received before taking the artifact. But he had to get to the bottom of this as soon as possible. Enough mystery was enough.

Jeremiah's dad's cell phone rang. *Great.* What now?

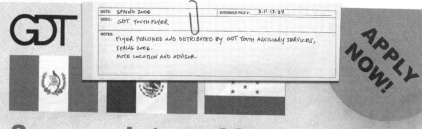

Summer internships in

 Latin America

GDT is sponsoring a limited number of internships to southern Mexico, Guatemala, and Honduras for the months of June and July.
Provide meaningful service this summer and:

* Tutor children in English and math

* Build sanitary water facilities

* Help plant and maintain sustainable gardens and cash crops

* Assist medical personnel in providing vaccinations and basic health care

This is your opportunity to see a little-known corner of the world while helping the less fortunate, enhancing your college resume, and raising your profile with a trans-global company dedicated to bettering society at all levels.

We at GDT call that a WIN-WIN!

Brenna Lanton, your local chapter leader, has all application materials available. Contact her for further information.

APPLICATION DEADLINE: MAY 1, 2006

CHAPTER THREE

Detour

Jeremiah's dad deftly fished his phone out of his pocket as he drove and answered it. Before he could say anything, a stream of high-pitched words spilled out of it. Jeremiah couldn't make sense of what they said, but he could tell by the tone that it wasn't the beginning of a casual chat. Roger cut off the barrage midstream.

"Well, you'll just have to start eating without us. See you in fifteen." He clicked the End button and handed his phone to his wife. "That woman—"

"Roger . . ." But Jeremiah knew that his mother spoke out of sympathy, not real reproach. His dad and Aunt Marilyn had never gotten along. As far as Jeremiah could tell, it was because they were too much alike: practical, hardheaded, organized, sure that their way was the right way, moving ahead with their own plans and expecting everyone else just to fall in line and follow without question. That kind of thing worked well when there was one person like that in the family—but with two? Family events had been garnished with tension over what to do and when for as long as Jeremiah could remember.

But right now, he wanted some answers to the fifty million questions buzzing around his head *before* they got to the reunion. He picked the one that seemed the most urgent and forged ahead. "So all of a sudden, I have a new birthday? I can't believe you guys have never told me. What's next? You're not my real parents?" He wanted to keep the mood light; his parents were both still visibly shaken after their encounter in the library.

But his mom didn't seem like she was going to be joked out of anything. She looked back, grief and regret in her eyes. "It's just not that simple, honey . . ."

His dad cut in, meeting Jeremiah's gaze in the rearview mirror. "Look, there's not enough time to explain everything. We're late, and Aunt Marilyn is already off on one of her—"

Jeremiah interrupted, even though he knew that drove his dad nuts. "*So?* Aunt Marilyn can wait. This is my life!"

His dad half turned as he drove and noticed that Jeremiah had his camera running. "Would you turn that thing off?"

Jeremiah sat back and pointedly raised the camera. "No."

"We should've gotten him a printer," his dad muttered.

Danger. Life or death. Jeremiah felt it even more strongly than before.

Again? What was going on this time? He couldn't recall a day in which he'd had more than one warning—and here he was, having them every few minutes. This was bizarre.

He tried to tell himself that he was just in shock, but the prompting welled up within him, undeniable. He put his hand on his mother's shoulder. He knew what he had to say wasn't going to fly, but he had to try.

"You guys are the ones who told me to listen to my promptings. Look, I can't tell you why, but we need to get out of Manti. Right now."

Debra twisted around in her seat. "You heard your dad. The later we are, the more unpleasant it's going to be. Let's make happy memories, okay?"

Jeremiah leaned forward, his voice thick with urgency. "I told you to pull over right before that truck almost ran us off the road, so why won't you listen to me now? We need to turn around. Right now."

His mother nodded at Jeremiah. She got it, he could tell. She looked over at her husband to get his attention. But his father stared straight ahead, and his white-knuckled grip on the steering wheel told Jeremiah that they weren't veering from the plan.

Jeremiah tried again in his most reasonable tone. "We're not safe. We need to get off the road." The feeling made his heart thud like it was going to burst out of his chest. Time to change strategies. How could he pull his dad off task?

Inspiration hit him. "Look, I need to use the restroom. We can all go. Mom, you always need to go."

His dad exhaled hard, as if forcing himself to relax. Then he laughed a little and pulled over next to the pumps of an old, decrepit-looking gas station on the next corner and sighed. He looked into the rearview mirror at Jeremiah. "You have ninety seconds."

Jeremiah got out of the minivan, his camera still on. He didn't really have to go to the bathroom, but he had to buy some time and figure out how to convince his parents not to go on to his grandparents' house. There was something wrong here in Manti; he felt sure of it. He closed the door, but then he paused. The woman at the library had told him to keep the box with him at all times. She'd seemed pretty serious about it. He trusted his parents, but he needed to keep his word. He reopened the door and grabbed the plastic bag.

"We can watch that," his mother protested.

"That's not what she told me," Jeremiah said firmly.

"You've already lost twenty seconds," his dad said. His mom smacked him on the shoulder and laughed. His dad laughed too, and waved Jeremiah toward the gas station's mini-mart. Dad could be ornery, but he never held a grudge.

Jeremiah caught them on film through the van's window, his parents laughing and looking at him with love in their eyes. His mom gave a playful wave. Jeremiah turned and walked across the pavement.

Inside the gas station's cramped, dusty office, he stopped. Something felt off here. He wondered whether he should go to a different place instead, but a quick glance outside showed no alternatives nearby. He walked slowly past the counter, looking at the clerk behind it the whole time. The man glared at him. Jeremiah didn't think he imagined the menace in his eyes. Who was he? Jeremiah almost felt like he knew him. He wanted to leave again, but thought that would look odd.

"I just need to know where your restroom is," he asked, half-expecting the man to kick him out. Sometimes you couldn't use a bathroom at a place like this without buying something. But the man just nodded toward a dingy door in the corner.

Inside the dank restroom, Jeremiah set the box in the ancient, rust-stained sink and gazed at himself in the warped mirror. The 40-watt bulb flickered unsteadily as he looked at his reflection. What was going on? He quieted his breathing and listened. There *was* danger, associated with this box— and his parents—but he couldn't see for the moment which way to turn. And why was it that he felt he should keep his video camera running the whole time?

The nasty smells in the tiny room were too distracting, and Jeremiah couldn't come to any clear decision. Finally, he took up the box and walked out. Again, under the sickly fluorescent lights, he felt a sense of oppression.

The clerk leered at him. "Who sent you?" he growled.

"I'm . . . looking for double salted licorice nips. My grandpa got me hooked, and I can only find them out here in the sticks." Jeremiah fingered a couple of plastic bags of junk food hanging from pegboard hooks above a shelf, pretending to consider a purchase. Everything in here looked faded and past its expiration date.

The man lowered his hat over his eyes and stepped back, out of the direct light. Where had Jeremiah seen him before?

Something nagged at the edge of his memory, but he came up with nothing.

"Why you bringin' a camera in here?" the man asked, his voice full of suspicion. His harsh tone raised Jeremiah's hackles.

Jeremiah lingered, hesitating. What was he supposed to do next? Right now, his discernment was failing him. He couldn't go back out to his parents, not yet. "Just looking for licorice nips," he said, stalling.

"Don't sell lick'rish. No snaps, whips, twists, or double salted." He glanced around, ferret-like, then peered out of the filthy windows, looking out at Jeremiah's parents' van. "Who sent you?" He snaked out from behind the counter toward Jeremiah and snatched at the plastic bag holding the box. "What's in the bag?" he yelled.

Jeremiah jerked hard on the bag, pulling it and the man toward him. He smelled chewing tobacco on the man's foul breath, so strong it nearly made him retch. He yanked at the bag again, desperate to get it out of the man's grasp. "Leave it alone!"

A huge crash deafened Jeremiah. His assailant let go of the sack in his shock and stumbled backward. The momentum sent Jeremiah careening into the door. He knocked his head hard on the safety glass, then recovered his balance. He looked outside. And screamed.

A semitruck sped away down the street, leaving in its wake the crumpled mass of metal that used to be the Whitneys' minivan. Smoke streamed out from under its hood and billowed up into the air.

"Mom! Dad!" Jeremiah yelled, charging out the door. He dropped his camera and the plastic bag and ran for the pumps, hoping against hope that his parents had left the van. He paused and looked back as he reached the gas pumps. The box. He wasn't supposed to leave it alone and out in the open. He took a half step back toward it, but then shook himself. What was he thinking? His parents were far more important right now. He brushed aside the twinge of guilt he felt and ran to the minivan, but when he reached it, his heart failed him.

His father lay slumped over the steering wheel, blood streaming from his head, and unconscious—at best. His mother, who must have taken off her seat belt while waiting for Jeremiah to return, had been thrown partway through the windshield. Her body and head were twisted so her sightless eyes stared up at the white winter sky.

Jeremiah tore around the side of the car to pull her from the wreckage. He tried to wrestle her body free, but it was no use. Her legs had been pinned under the dashboard by the impact.

Suddenly, strong arms from behind ripped him from his mother's side and carried him several yards from the car. He fought against the person restraining him but couldn't wrench free. A voice muttered in his ear. "That car's going to go up—and the pumps and tanks might go with it." Seconds later, his words came true. The minivan exploded in a ball of fire. Jeremiah could only feel the depth of his screams as all sound was muffled by the blast.

His rescuer released him. Jeremiah sank to his knees on

the icy asphalt, unable to look away from the horrific sight of his parents' bodies burning. Sirens wailed in the distance, but Jeremiah was numb to all that now.

Fire trucks arrived and miraculously put out the blaze before it could spread to the underground pumps. The police questioned him for what seemed like hours. Why had his family stopped at the gas station? Why had Jeremiah left the car? What was his business here? Had he seen the license plate of the truck that had rammed into the van?

Through a haze, he heard a resident from across the street tell what she saw. "It just came out of nowhere, going full speed, like it was out on the highway and not on a town street. At the last second, it swerved and hit that van. I thought maybe it moved to avoid someone in the street, but there was no one there. Now that I think about it, that truck must have hit that van on purpose. Like someone planned for this to happen. And the truck didn't have any license plates—at least none I could see."

Jeremiah sat with a blanket wrapped around his shoulders. His parents were gone, just like that. He'd argued with them minutes before. Now he'd never see them again—not in this lifetime.

He yearned to see his last image of them again, and felt around his shoulders for the strap of his camera. It wasn't there—and he remembered his struggle with the gas station attendant.

He leapt from the edge of the ambulance where he'd been sitting and ran around the taped-off accident scene, toward the gas station's office. He must have dropped the camera on the pavement. Sure enough, just outside the door, he found it—still recording, even. He was amazed at the battery life.

The box he had been given at the library. Where was it? He had seen it right there. Search as he might in the fading light, though, he knew within his heart that he'd lost it. Minutes after having been given a mysterious sacred trust, he had proved himself untrustworthy.

That stupid box. If they hadn't stopped for it—if they had gone on to his grandparents' house the way his father had wanted to—his parents would still be alive. Wouldn't they?

Maybe that's why his father had been so insistent that they keep going—maybe he had had a potentially life-saving prompting of his own. Maybe that was why Jeremiah had been so confused when he was in the gas station restroom. Maybe this time, he had been wrong.

Jeremiah shook his head, sick with regret. He saw now that he was more like his father than he had thought; his way was the only right way. He had been so positive that his promptings would lead them to safety. But his father was the patriarch of their family; shouldn't he be the one who would be entitled to those promptings? Jeremiah had always been so sure that he knew better. Not anymore.

Overwhelmed by grief, Jeremiah faced the truth: he had caused his parents' deaths, as surely as if he had driven that truck himself.

Jeremiah allowed a policeman to lead him toward a car. Numbly, he got in and leaned his head on the vinyl headrest in the backseat. He felt grateful for the refuge. The local authorities had wrung every detail from every witness who had seen (or hadn't seen) anything pertaining to the horrific "accident." Reporters milled around the scene, talking to locals and taking video as a tow truck hauled the blackened mess that had once been the Whitneys' minivan onto its flat bed. The bodies had been taken away by ambulance hours before.

The irony of that stung Jeremiah. Why was an emergency vehicle necessary to transport the remains, when there was no hope that anything could be done for them? But Jeremiah realized it was just procedure.

The officer who had questioned Jeremiah so closely now slid into the driver's seat and turned around to face him.

"Would you like us to take you to your grandparents' house?"

"No." Jeremiah's relatives had all come to the scene as soon as they heard, but the police wouldn't let them speak to Jeremiah. He wasn't a suspect, the police said, but they needed him to remember everything he could for their reports. They assured his family they would release him as soon as possible.

Finally, his devastated grandparents and aunt had driven back home. Jeremiah's phone kept beeping, and he knew that various relatives were trying to reach him. But he couldn't stand the thought of seeing them right now. He was afraid if they looked into his eyes, they would know the truth—that he *had* killed his parents. He couldn't bear that thought, not now.

No, it would be better to go back to Provo, back to the

relatively anonymous safety of the dorms. People would basically leave him alone there. He could collapse and stay unconscious for as long as possible—without well-meaning adults trying to get him to eat or talk or anything else.

"Everything okay?" the policeman asked.

Jeremiah nodded.

"We'll take you back to the university, then."

Jeremiah nodded again, and the police cruiser rolled north through the night. Restless, Jeremiah went back over the footage the camera had recorded until he found the frame that had captured his parents, smiling and waving as he left them to go into the gas station. He stared down into their laughing, loving eyes, unable to believe that they were gone. Just then, the camera's battery finally died, and Jeremiah felt a little piece of his heart die with it.

Outside his dorm, Jeremiah got out of the car without thanking the officers, and headed inside. As the cruiser turned around, the lights of a dark sedan turned on in the driveway opposite.

Jeremiah stopped on the porch outside the door to his dorm, hoping he could avoid as many friends and acquaintances as possible once he went inside.

The wind gusted around him, and on it came a faint whisper. "Massasoit," it seemed to say.

What? Jeremiah whipped around. Had someone just spoken to him? What had the voice said? But no one was there. The hair on the back of his neck stood up again, but he ignored it. He was too tired for this.

He climbed the same steps he had ascended just hours

before with his parents. With each one, he regretted every time he'd deliberately gotten on his father's nerves, every time he'd suffered through one of his mother's countless, and sometimes annoying, hugs. They were both gone now, and those moments he'd taken for granted seemed more precious than he could possibly have imagined.

On the second floor landing, his phone buzzed—but it wasn't another one of his relatives. Instead, he had received a text from an unknown sender. "You must be worthy of the box."

Was this some kind of joke? Someone had stolen the box after he had consciously abandoned it so that he could try to save his parents. Was this from whoever had taken it? If so, how had they gotten his phone number?

Outside the door of his dorm room, Jeremiah halted and listened. *Ugh.* His next-door neighbors, Simon and Brian, were inside, probably playing the latest fantasy role-playing game with Porter. He didn't know how they ever got any actual studying done. *Whatever.* He opened the door and eased around them all and past Porter's giant armchair without acknowledging any of them. Hopefully they would get the message and leave him alone.

His parents were gone, and it was all his fault. He had been given a sacred trust and had promptly abandoned it. He didn't think he would ever be able to forgive himself. His despair was so thick it nauseated him. How could he possibly go on with his life after what had happened today?

TE: OB DECEMBER 2008

SC.: INSURANCE DAMAGE CLAIM

EVIDENCE FILE #: 5.1.5.50

TES EXCERPT FROM A DAMAGE CLAIM FILED BY SANPETE HEAVY EQUIPMENT
RENTALS, WITH ZION'S INSURANCE UNDERWRITERS.
SECURITY CAMERA FOOTAGE MISSING FROM RENTAL COMPANY.

SECTION 1. ACCIDENT SUMMARY	
INCIDENT DATE:	December 8, 2008
INCIDENT TYPE:	Vehicle theft, damage, and subsequent abandonment

SECTION 2. VEHICLE INFORMATION	
TYPE OF VEHICLE:	Freightliner Heavy Duty Cab
YEAR AND MODEL OF VEHICLE:	2005 Cascadia

SECTION 3. DAMAGE INFORMATION	
DAMAGE SUSTAINED:	Front right fender crumpled and half torn off; front grill smashed. Damage to electrical system, consistent with "hot-wiring."
REPAIR ESTIMATE:	$11,500
INCIDENT DESCRIPTION:	Truck stolen from rental lot and discovered abandoned near county line several hours later.
OTHER VEHICLES INVOLVED?	Possibly. See below.
POLICE REPORT FILED?	Yes. Possible connection to same day fatal hit-and-run in Manti being investigated. Deputy Ramsey at Sanpete County Sheriff's Office will provide further details.

SECTION 4. COMMENTS	
ADDITIONAL INFORMATION:	Witnesses saw vehicle slam into minivan owned by Roger Whitney. Roger Whitney and wife, Deborah, were killed instantly upon impact.

CHAPTER FOUR

Porter's Call

"Brian, orcs can't do that!" Simon yelled. Porter winced as Simon's tortured squawks grated on his eardrums. Simon looked like a crazy man after a couple of hours spent on the new expansion of his favorite role-playing game. He had pulled his wild, red hair into a frenzied Afro in his stress, and his saucer-like blue eyes were bloodshot. Porter shifted onto his other elbow, careful not to knock over the game board with its dozens of carefully arranged playing pieces.

He had to admit that the game expansion was cool, but boredom had begun to set in. He idly wondered what his girlfriend Lilah was doing and resolved to text her soon.

Porter waited for Brian's response to Simon's protest and felt tempted to make a snarky comment about how the three of them were wedged here between his and Jeremiah's beds, playing with little dolls—albeit with battle axes and spears—just to yank Simon's chain for awhile. That would liven things up a bit.

"He's not an orc." Brian pushed up his glasses as he

replied in his most condescending tone. "He's only disguised as one. I have a conspiracy card."

Heh, thought Porter. *Good one. Par for the course with Brian.* He watched as Brian rearranged a grouping of the tiny pewter figures.

"There is no such card," cried Simon, outraged. A stickler for the complicated rules, he hated it when his roommate tried to cheat—or "play outside the box," as Brian called it.

Brian cackled, looking even more like a frog than usual. "That's the thing about conspiracies. You don't even know they exist."

Porter looked up as Jeremiah came in and stepped over their sprawled bodies to cross their tiny dorm room. He looked gray with exhaustion and seemed to be avoiding everyone's eyes. He also had dirt or something smudged on his face. What had he been up to?

"Help me," Porter muttered at him with a rueful grin, hoping Jeremiah would get the joke and rescue him from these two. Maybe then they could go out and get some ice cream. But Jeremiah looked away instead.

Brian jumped up at once when he saw Jeremiah, the orc campaign forgotten for the moment. He shoved a paper under Jeremiah's nose. "Look at what somebody did to my flyers," he said. "I found this in the trash. They blacked out the dates and everything. Someone doesn't want Dr. Davenport here."

Porter bit off a retort. He and Jeremiah had suffered through dozens of Brian's endless monologues about secret combinations and "scenarios" and "black hats" over the past semester. Why was Brian bringing this up now? Jeremiah hardly seemed in the mood to endure another one. Porter switched to distraction mode as he moved to the rescue.

"Probably the orcs, right, Simon?" If he could rouse the wannabe elf to join him in the attack, he could get Conspiracy Boy off Jeremiah's back.

Jeremiah dropped his new camera case and his backpack on the floor and curled up on his bed, facing the wall.

"Jeremiah, we were just storming the castle," Simon announced hopefully. Porter knew that Simon preferred playing with four or more players and would hound Jeremiah to join them. It was time for drastic action. Porter tipped over the game board in a crash of plastic and little bits of metal.

"Oops. War's over. Bye, guys."

Porter knew that his neighbors, as clueless as they were, wouldn't mistake his commanding tone. Simon scurried to pick everything up, making sure he didn't lose a single precious game piece. He shuffled all of his equipment together and moved to the door with Brian.

"Mark my words," Brian said as he slouched out. "Someone is watching. I can smell these things."

His last words were muffled; Porter had shut the door in his face. He turned and regarded his roommate's seemingly unconscious form. Why the pouting? Something was wrong here. Porter knew how to fix that.

Step one: some of his patented teasing.

Step two: ice cream. The expensive kind.

"Mommy didn't give you a good night kiss?" Porter

sing-songed, trying to get a rise out of Jeremiah. No response.

"You all right, Jer?" he asked after a moment. "Happy birthday."

Dang. Porter didn't want to go get ice cream alone. That was just pathetic. He looked at his roommate, who seemed to have gone all comatose. What had happened at that stupid family reunion? Was it just tryptophan overload from too many helpings of turkey? Or had Jeremiah gotten into an argument? That would be a drag—on his birthday, no less. It wouldn't surprise Porter, though. From what Jeremiah had told him, the Whitney family seemed to have its fair share of drama.

Whatever it was, Jeremiah wasn't ready to talk about it. No matter. Porter would ferret it out of him eventually. He wasn't a direct descendant of Porter Rockwell for nothing. He could be patient. He could wait.

Something was off, though; Porter felt jumpy, and not just from ice cream cravings. He squeezed between Jeremiah's desk and bed and peeked out through the closed blinds of their window.

Sure enough, his feeling was dead on. Someone watched them from across the way. There was no mistaking it; this guy had what looked like night vision binoculars and a big cup of coffee, like he was on a stakeout or something. *So not cool.* Why would somebody be spying on a couple of college freshmen? Porter usually rolled his eyes at Brian's wacky theories, but right now, he felt like he was smack in the middle of one unfolding.

The guy sat in the driver's seat of the generic-looking car and yapped on a bluetooth stuck in his ear as he fiddled with his equipment. Porter hated bluetooths. *Blueteeth? Who knew?* The guy's binoculars were probably hi-res enough to see Porter peeking through the blinds—and what if they had infrared? Porter's big frame would be lit up like a Christmas tree. He suddenly felt very vulnerable.

As he let the blind go, a wave of fear hit him from out of nowhere. Something was very wrong—and it had to do with whatever Jeremiah had been doing this evening. He got goose bumps on the back of his neck as he looked down at his roommate. What had happened?

"Keep him on the straight and narrow." A whisper reverberated throughout the room. Jeremiah lay silent and showed no sign of having heard. "You can protect him."

Great. I'm hearing voices. Here's where I officially go crazy. Brian has infected me.

But this felt real, and it felt important. Porter sat on the edge of his bed and listened; the voice came again. It sounded just like Jeremiah's mother, echoing her very words that afternoon. "He's my only son. Take care of him."

What was going on? Was he having some kind of hallucination? This was not normal, not at all. Why would Sister Whitney be speaking to him through supernatural means?

"You can do it, Porter; help him. You're all he's got now."

Warmth and peace flooded Porter's chest, a sensation he hadn't experienced often—not since his mission, anyway.

He picked up a blanket from the foot of his bed and draped it over Jeremiah. There. That was helpful, right? *What now?* Feeling directed—not knowing what he was doing beforehand—he heaved his giant, dilapidated armchair over in front of the door and flopped down in it. If anyone wanted to get to Jeremiah, they'd have to go through him first—and that would take some doing.

He took the afghan Lilah had crocheted for him last Christmas and slung it over his shoulders. Staring at Jeremiah, he heard the voice again: "Keep him safe." Porter could do that. Protecting people was in his DNA. Suddenly exhausted, Porter closed his eyes and dreamed.

• • •

He stood sweating in his dark suit in the hot sun, waiting for his junior comp to knock on the door. Elder Whitney was taking his sweet time about it. Whitney shifted his backpack to the other shoulder and shuffled the pamphlets in his hand, then finally reached out and rapped on the weathered wood.

"Took you long enough," Porter muttered.

Whitney gave him a look, but said nothing. They'd been tracting for hours in the oppressive eastern heat. This was Porter's second summer in upstate New York, but he still hadn't gotten used to the thick humidity. No wonder his ancestors had gone west. He felt sweat running down his back and pooling above his tightly cinched belt. He hoped that someone would let them in soon—preferably someone with lemonade and air conditioning.

That probably wasn't going to happen, not in this neighborhood. It was a group of sad little Cape Cod-style houses wrapped in 50-year-old aluminum siding in various shades of mildewed white, puke green, and faded, anemic yellow. These were the kind of yards that had cars up on spider-webbed concrete blocks and long-dead appliances sitting under scrubby, weedy trees like forgotten party guests. It didn't look all that welcoming. But, Porter admitted, he'd been wrong many times before. They wouldn't give up—not yet.

Whitney knocked on the door again, but it seemed that no one was home. Or at least, no one was willing to come to the door and reject them in person. Porter loved serving the Lord, but tracting had always felt to him like a huge waste of a missionary's time.

"Let's go, Elder," he said to his junior companion, and they carefully descended the broken concrete steps of the little house.

But then he heard a creak behind him. He and Whitney turned at the same time, only to see purple-skinned orcs with hideous tattoos piling out of the house and crowding onto the tiny front stoop. Each one brandished a wicked, hooked sword and wore not much else besides a breechclout.

What the heck?

Porter looked down to find that instead of scriptures and tracts, he now held a long, jeweled sword and fancy, heavy shield. He chanced a sideways glance at his companion, who also held weapons and stared at them as if he had no idea what to do with them.

Screeching bloody murder, the orcs descended, and Porter and Whitney fell back, raising their weapons and defending themselves as well as they could. Porter's time in the Society of Creative Anachronism had paid off; he fared slightly better than Whitney. He parried and thrusted, drawing black blood every once in a while, grunting and yelling and doing his best to give as good as he got. It was hot, sweaty work. No one ever mentioned that when they told the story of Ammon at the water's edge, did they?

Whitney dropped his sword and ducked behind Porter. Porter stole half a look behind him as he hacked off an orc's head, which spurted black ichor everywhere; Whitney was rummaging through his backpack.

"This is not the time for a snack, Elder!" he yelled, but Whitney wasn't getting out the beef jerky. Instead, he pulled out a rustic-looking wooden box with weird designs on it. He turned, jumped in front of Porter, and stood with his legs spread wide, holding the box up high over his head. He looked for all the world like some hero in a video game. As he raised the box, bolts of lightning shot out of it at their foes, vaporizing each into stinky violet mists, one after the other.

Finally, all the orcs were gone, nothing remaining but a few dismembered arms on the ground, still holding the curved blades.

"What is that thing, Elder?" Porter asked in wonderment.

Elder Whitney looked down at the box in his hands. "I

have no idea." He looked at his companion. "I've never seen it before."

"Wicked cool weapon," Porter observed.

"Yeah." Their swords had disappeared, and their scriptures and pamphlets lay scattered on the ground. The two missionaries picked up any of the handouts that weren't spattered with orc guts and dusted off their quads.

"Okay, next house is yours, Elder Coolbrith," Whitney said, wiping sweat from his brow.

"Absolutely," Porter answered, and they moved on down the sidewalk.

Latter-day Saints is found in Manti and dominates the area's skyline.

According to the United States Census Bureau, the city has a total area of 2.0 square miles, all of it land.

Manti is located in a semi-arid climate with warm summers and cold winters. Its high elevation means that the climate is cooler than other populated areas of Utah, especially during summer. Summers highs average in the mid-80s°F, with winter highs in the mid-30s°F. Winter lows, however, dip to around 15-20°F.

Manti serves as the county seat of Sanpete County, Utah, United States. The population was 460 at the 1960 United States Census.

MASSASOIT Sachem or Ousamequin (c. 1581 – 1661) was the sachem, or leader, of the Wampanoag, and "Massasoit" of the Wampanoag Confederacy. The term Massasoit means Great Sachem.

Massasoit (Ousamequin) was born in Montaup, a Pokanoket village at the site of today's Warren and Bristol, Rhode Island. His residence was there near an abundant spring of water which still bears his name. He held the allegiance of seven lesser Wampanoag -

Fig. 1 **MASSASOIT EMERGES FROM HIS LODGE TO MEET WITH THE ENGLISH**

sachems. In March 1621, three months after the founding of Plymouth, an Abenaki by the name Samoset entered the town and exclaimed in English—which he had learned from the Penobscot fishermen and from the English fishermen that came to fish off Monhegan Island—"Welcome, Englishmen!" He announced himself as the envoy of Massasoit, "the greatest commander of the country."

After some negotiation, Massasoit came in person and was received with due ceremony. Massasoit negotiated a treaty guaranteeing the English their security in exchange for their alliance against the Narragansett. Both parties promised to abstain from mutual injuries and to deliver offenders; the colonists were to

Fig. 2 **MASSASOIT STATUE**

recieve asistance if attacked, to render it if Massasoit should be unjustly assailed. Massasoit actively sought the alliance ever since two significant outbreaks of smallpox brought by the English had devastated the Wampanoag during the previous six years. The tribe was devastated by the influx of English diseases. The treaty included the confederates of the sachem, and was sacredly kept for Massasoit's lifetime.

Though he was commonly known as Massasoit, in fact he was called by many other and divers names, including: Ousamequin, Woosamequin, Asuhmequin, Oosamequen, Osamekin, Owsameguin, Owsamequine, and

CHAPTER FIVE

The Departure

"Freeze!" Porter said as he jumped awake. Someone was on the attack yet again, but his sword seemed to have disappeared. *Dang.* He looked up blearily from his recliner. *Gah.* He had a horrible crick in his neck from sleeping in the velour-covered thing all night—and his left foot had fallen asleep. *What the crap?* Why had he thought this was a good idea? Struggling, he levered the footrest back into the body of the chair and sat up.

Jeremiah stood over him, towel and toothbrush in hand, looking annoyed. "Hey. I need to brush my teeth."

"Oh. Right." Porter got up and shoved his chair to the side. Jeremiah brushed past without saying a word and left the room. *Seriously?* How could he just ignore him like this, after all they'd been through together? Porter removed his blanket from Jeremiah's bed and threw it across the room. Rubbing his eyes, he sat down. That dream had felt so real—but of course he and Jeremiah hadn't been mission companions. Jeremiah had just turned eighteen—he wouldn't be going on his mission for another year, the young'un.

Crazy stuff—those orcs, that box. He shook his head to banish the intense memory of the battle—and the putrid stench of frying orc. He didn't remember ever having dreamed a smell. Was that even possible? Maybe Lilah would know. Sniffing under his arm, he woke up fully. *Speaking of stink. Yikes.* He grabbed his own towel and headed to the shower.

An hour later, Porter entered into the cafeteria, after meeting Lilah outside. Porter loved walking around campus with her on his arm. She was so beautiful that other guys always gave him looks of grudging respect once they peeled their eyes off of her. With her ivory skin and supermodel frame, she could have dated any guy in the valley. But she had chosen Porter. He didn't exactly get it, but he was grateful.

Plus, Lilah was smart and practical—and calm under pressure. He could always count on her to come through with wisdom and grace.

"See, there he is," he said, pointing out Jeremiah to her. He was sitting and eating by himself. "I'm so ticked at him, I can't even tell you. He didn't even say 'good night.' Usually I can't get him to shut up, which really affects my grades."

Lilah looked up at Porter, her big, dark eyes full of laughter. She brushed her long, perfectly straight black hair behind her shoulders, then stood on tiptoe and kissed his cheek. "Well, you just have to rise above it, right, sweetie?" She squeezed his arm encouragingly. "You're only seven credits away from being a sophomore. I'm really proud of how hard you've been working." She nudged him playfully. "Come on. Let's go talk to him."

They walked over and slid into the booth where Jeremiah sat shoveling oatmeal into his mouth with diligence and focus.

Porter leaned on his forearms and looked at his roommate, who seemed to be ignoring him yet again. He felt heat rise in his face. "So, Jeremiah. I don't appreciate—" He felt a pinch on his arm and looked at Lilah. She raised a perfectly arched eyebrow at him. *Right.* He had to take this slowly. But what should he say now?

Lilah filled in the gap for him. "How's your oatmeal?"

Jeremiah looked up at her with half a polite smile. At least he'd make eye contact with her.

Porter tried again. "You know, my Great-great-great-great-great Grandpa Rockwell said that a real man sprinkles a little bit of gunpowder on his oatmeal every day." He paused. No reaction. "Of course, when they cremated him, he made a fifteen-foot hole in the wall."

Lilah laughed even though she'd heard the joke before. She was always an awesome audience. Jeremiah even grinned a bit. *Good.* Porter felt like progress had been made. "So, uh, how'd you get home last night? There was this weird car out front."

"Oh." Jeremiah chewed his bite of oatmeal for far longer than seemed necessary. "You know, I bet that was probably just my uncle."

Porter stared at his roommate. What, did Jeremiah think he was mentally challenged or something? Why would his uncle sit outside the dorm in a dark car, fooling around with all kinds of expensive spy equipment? Why couldn't Jay think up a more convincing lie?

He was formulating a scathing response when a cute coed walked up to their table. She didn't seem to see Porter and Lilah and stared at Jeremiah as if working up the courage to speak. It was no wonder; with his dark hair, blue eyes, and high cheekbones, Jeremiah had looks that seemed to attract the womenfolk—even though Porter privately thought he was a little on the scrawny side.

"You probably don't even remember me, but . . ." The coed bent down to catch Jeremiah's eye. "I'm in your ward?" She said it like it was a question. Porter hated it when girls did that. Wasn't she sure? But she was very cute—wavy, golden-brown hair, puppy-dog-brown eyes—so Porter decided to give her the benefit of the doubt.

When Jeremiah made no sign of recognizing her, the girl continued. "Anyway, I just wanted to say that I heard about last night, and I wanted to say sorry. . . . I'm so sorry." Her voice roughened with sympathy and concern. This was more than some chick trying to score a date. Porter looked at his roommate to gauge his reaction.

Jeremiah blanched like he was going to be sick or something—the way he had looked last night when he had come home. Porter stared back at the girl. What had happened last night? Had Jeremiah gotten himself into some kind of trouble? And how had she found out about it?

"Claire!" Another girl stood at the other end of the booth, like she had materialized out of nowhere. Who was this skank? She looked *narsty* with a capital "R." Her skin-tight

designer jeans looked like they had been spray-painted on.
Porter should report her to the standards board. They were
topped with a fancy, expensive-looking sweater. She grinned
at Jeremiah with gleaming, Osmond-white dental work. She
set Porter's teeth on edge, and she'd only said one word.

She remedied that in a heartbeat, though. "Claire," she
said, addressing the cute girl. "I just wanted to thank you
again for setting up that Kirby Heyborne interview. You are
just learning so fast!"

There was something utterly fake about that smile
of hers; it was more like a snarl. She glanced at everyone
else seated at the table. "I'm sorry; I'm being rude," she
said, sliding across the bench and scooching right up next
to Jeremiah. Porter could smell her French perfume from
across the table. *Subtle touch.*

"I'm Megan Halling." She paused as if introducing
herself further were totally unnecessary. When no one re-
sponded, she frowned slightly and spoke more slowly,
as if they were all idiots. "You've probably seen me on
zoobynews.com. I'm Claire's mentor." Looking up at the
cute girl, she asked, "Who are these people, Claire?"

Claire stuttered a bit, obviously intimidated. Porter
wanted to shake her and tell her to grow a backbone. She
was worth ten of "Zooby News star" Megan Halling; Porter
could see that just by looking at her.

"Well, this is Jeremiah . . ."

Megan cut her off. "The one you always talk about?"

Claire blushed, turning redder than any girl Porter had
ever seen. *Interesting.*

"What do you mean?" she sputtered lamely, but Porter was on to her now. She *liked* Jay. *Fantastic.* The man needed a cute girl to pull him out of his funk. Porter could work with this.

"Don't be silly," Megan said, and turned to Jeremiah. In a hushed, melodramatic tone, she spoke while stroking his forearm. "How are you holding up? Your story—it broke my heart."

What? Porter looked at Lilah for guidance; she always knew what was going on in social situations when he did not. But for once, she looked as clueless as he felt. Jeremiah kept his eyes down and said nothing. Porter hated that this bimbo knew something about his roommate that he himself did not.

"What story, Jay?" Porter forced a chuckle. "D'you win the lottery or something?"

Megan looked at him as if he were an insect. She checked the incredulous smile spreading across her face and shoved a newspaper under Porter's nose.

COUPLE KILLED IN CRASH, SECOND DRIVER MISSING. In the photo under the headline, Jeremiah stood near the burning hulk of an automobile. Porter's heart dropped into his stomach. This could not be happening. But it made sense now—the way Jay had come in last night and collapsed without speaking to anyone.

Porter suddenly felt ashamed for being irritated with his friend. But why hadn't Jeremiah trusted him enough to confide in him? Porter felt betrayed, but wondered how he had failed his friend at the same time. "Jeremiah. Why didn't you tell us?"

Lilah reached across the table and took Jeremiah's hand. Porter glanced at her and could see tears welling up in her gorgeous eyes.

"You didn't know?" Megan said, clearly gleeful that she'd scooped Porter. Oh, she was so disgusting. Porter wanted to punch something. "Aren't you supposed to be his roommate?"

Porter had to keep himself from mimicking her sneering, fake reproach back at her. He watched as she turned the paper around again and scrutinized the photo. Then she looked at Jeremiah and caught sight of the camera strap around his neck. "Did you have this camera on you when the accident happened?" she asked, tugging on the bag. Jeremiah pulled it out of her grasp and shied away toward the opposite end of the booth. Megan leaned after him.

"A semi killed your parents and got away with it."

"Megan!" Claire interrupted in a shocked tone, but Megan was apparently shameless.

"You've got to come on my show and set the record straight. If you have footage from that tragedy, I can use my position to apprehend the murderer—"

Porter had had enough. He leaned forward to get Megan's eye. "Look, I don't allow him to be interviewed by trollop journalists, so back off."

Megan glared at him, but Jeremiah started gathering his things and broke their staring match. "I've got to go," he said. Megan backed out of the booth to let him past. He reached under the table and grabbed a small carry-on suitcase.

"Jeremiah—" Lilah said, but Megan cut her off.

Clutching Jeremiah's arm, she said, "Your parents deserve justice. Is there anything you want to say about the accident?" He shook his arm loose and started walking away. Porter stumbled over Lilah to catch Jeremiah before he left the cafeteria. "Dude, where are you going?" Jeremiah looked at him; Porter saw that he was pleading for understanding and support, even though his words were brusque. "To a funeral," he said. Porter grabbed his arm, but Jeremiah twisted out of his grasp. "The airport shuttle is waiting," he said blankly.

Then he turned and walked toward the bank of glass doors. Dumbfounded, Porter watched him go. Last night, a voice had told him to protect Jeremiah, but he hadn't been able to do that. Not so far. Not in his crazy dream, and not in reality—which was feeling more and more like a nightmare.

The hussy reporter and her cute underling had disappeared. Porter turned back to Lilah. "What am I supposed to do now?"

"All we can do now is pray for him. I can't imagine his pain," she said. "When he gets back, we'll figure the rest of it out. Right, honey?"

"Right." What would he do without Lilah? Porter didn't ever want to find out. She was the best. Looking down at her, he returned her smile. Then his stomach rumbled, breaking the romance of the moment. He realized that his appetite had returned in full force, like the faithful friend it had always been. "Now, let's get some breakfast. I'm starving."

Junk | Mark as ▾ | Move to ▾ | 🖨 ⬆⬇

Secret Combination Docs
  Probation status redaction
on landing hoax? Or extra-terrestrial cover-up?

ssages

ply all Forward

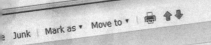

Secret Combination Docs

: trustno1.brian@trillomail.com
: Dec. 10, 2008
  fishystuff@netmail.net

g, you idiot! Don't forward this kind of stuff without scrubbing it first,
then using at LEAST a keyed Copiale-type cipher AND a secure
nnel. What would Prof. D. think?!? Next time, just go lo-tech/off-grid
d dead-drop it in my mailbox. I know you can't mess THAT up.

DATE: 10 DECEMBER 2008

EVIDENCE FILE #: 3.14.8.19

DESC.: INTERCEPTED EMAIL

NOTES: WHO IS GREG?

CHAPTER SIX

Coming Home

The long flight to Seneca Falls felt like a blur. Jeremiah had transferred at Newark for a much smaller plane that would take him to Finger Lakes Regional Airport. Now, as he touched down on one of the narrow runways there, his most recent hometown looked like a foreign country. Encrusted in dirty ice, skeletal trees sticking up out of the frozen wastes—you'd think he was in the Arctic, not upstate New York. The plane came to a stop, and Jeremiah made his way down the wheeled steps in the bitter air. His parents' bishop was there on the tarmac to greet him and take him home. The Whitneys had no family in Seneca Falls and had only lived there for three years, but Jeremiah knew that the ward would take care of him while he was there.

Bishop Freeman didn't talk much under the best of circumstances; he was an electrician and worked with his hands all day. Jeremiah actually preferred that. Talking was highly overrated, especially in situations like this. They rode in silence to Jeremiah's house.

Once they had stopped at the top of the long driveway the bishop put a rough hand on Jeremiah's shoulder and broke his silence. "I'm so sorry, son," he said. "We don't know the Lord's plans for us, do we? Your parents were good people, though. I know you'll miss them, but you'll see them again someday. I bear you my testimony of that."

Jeremiah nodded, the lump in his throat preventing him from speaking for a moment. Finally, he took a deep breath, managed a whispered, "Thanks," and got out of the battered pick-up truck.

He unlocked the front door and turned on the thermostat. His parents had been here only a couple of days ago. After dropping his bag off in his room, he felt unbearably lonely. Why had he come back? There was another service being held next week in Manti at Grandpa and Grandma Whitney's ward. He'd be surrounded by family and friends who'd known him since he was very small.

But the Seneca Falls Ward, shocked at the sudden death of their high priests group leader and Primary chorister, had wanted to have more than just a simple graveside service here as well. Jeremiah couldn't begrudge them that.

Before the funeral on Saturday, he had a ton to do. Among other things, he would have to go through his parents' belongings and pack them up. He'd leave the sale of the house to his parents' lawyer to handle—but their personal effects? As his parents' only child, he was the one who should take care of those things. It was his duty, he reminded himself. That's why he was here. It wasn't for him; it was for them.

He walked through the empty, quiet rooms, flipping on every light switch he passed. He turned on the television and the stereo too, hoping to fill up the emptiness with warmth and noise and light.

In the kitchen, he opened the fridge out of habit. He didn't feel hungry, but knew he should probably eat something. His parents had only planned to be gone a few days, so there should be plenty to choose from. Since Jeremiah had gone to college, his mom had become an empty nester, but she loved having people over for dinner and always wanted to be ready to take a meal to someone in need. Yeah, food shouldn't be a problem.

He pushed past a carton of juice on the fridge's main shelf, and as he did so, a small piece of paper fluttered to the floor.

He bent and picked it up.

Hi, Sweetie! I love you!

It was a note in his father's handwriting. Tears filled Jeremiah's eyes. His father had always done that—tucked little scraps of paper with a few words scrawled on them in places where he and his mother would eventually find them. In his lunchbox, in the pocket of his Sunday suit jacket— they popped up everywhere. He'd never seen his father plant them, but he found them all the time. Weeks into the semester, he'd found them in random books, in his shaving kit, and other odd places. Jeremiah wondered whether he would ever find them all.

He crumpled the note and shoved it into his pocket. He

would save it; he always saved the notes. But looking at this one right now hurt too much.

He grabbed the juice and a couple of cheese sticks and went into the dining room. Sitting at his usual spot at the table, he stared at his reflection in the sliding glass door and wondered how he would ever get through the next few days.

• • •

The week turned out to be something of a blur. Jeremiah slept late every day, then halfheartedly sorted through dresser drawers and file cabinets, pulling the documents he knew to be most important out and putting them in his backpack. Why there? He didn't know; it just seemed like the safest place, since he carried it and his camera bag everywhere.

What was he afraid of?

He decided it didn't matter. Though he found himself in a fog, he felt led through it, slowly and gently. The Relief Society presidency came over on Thursday and packed up most of the food in the kitchen and a lot of the Whitneys' clothes. They thanked Jeremiah for his donation and assured him that it would all go to needy people in the ward. That afternoon, he boxed up some photo albums and scrapbooks his mother had assembled and mailed them to Manti. He knew those pictures would be doubly precious to his grandparents now.

As he was sorting through things, Jeremiah found his mother's sewing box. Inside, nestled beneath thread and pincushions and scissors, lay several old snapshots of him as a baby and young boy. With a lump rising in his throat, he slowly shuffled through them, sometimes looking at the dates and other notes his mother had written on the backs in ballpoint pen. Why weren't these in one of the scrapbooks?

"First trout, Haystack Lake, 1994"

The last photo was of him and his mother at the water's edge. Four-year-old Jeremiah held up a small fish on a line, his excited grin telegraphing his accomplishment. His mother knelt at his side, her smile just as happy and proud. Letting the photo slip out of his fingers, Jeremiah put his head down on his knees and sobbed.

His mother had always taken joy in his accomplishments and ached with him over his griefs. Jeremiah supposed that all mothers did that, but it had always seemed that she had a special gift for feeling the ups and downs of his life as least as deeply as he did. Now, he keenly felt her lack—that bond of shared emotion was no longer an immediate presence in the background of his days.

He had heard that amputees still sensed their missing arms or legs—"ghost limbs," he thought they were called. With his parents gone, he felt like a part of himself had been ripped away, but as he went through their belongings, he could pretend they might still walk into the room at any given moment.

At one point on Friday, though, he looked around at the messes he'd made here and there throughout the house and gave up. It was too much for one person to organize in a matter of hours. He had discovered that his dad had stowed a few hundred dollars in cash in his sock drawer. Jeremiah decided to use it to hire movers to box everything else up and put it in a storage unit for now. He'd deal with it all later—maybe when winter semester was over and he had had a little time to deal with his grief.

• • •

Saturday finally arrived. The funeral was . . . nice. The speakers did a fine job capturing what they knew about Roger and Debra Whitney—their willing service, their strong testimonies, their deep love for one another. The choir and a couple of soloists sang hymns of comfort and peace. Jeremiah sat on the front pew in a daze, grateful that no one seemed to expect much of him.

Afterward, when he had endured countless hugs and handshakes, Jeremiah refused all offers of transportation and walked the three miles home. It was a straight shot down Route 414 to his parents' house. Of everyone in the spread-out ward, the Whitneys had lived the closest to the chapel. They'd kept the extra key to the church's front door, and it was always Jeremiah's dad who got called to run over and turn out a bathroom light or grab something someone had forgotten. He'd been happy to help; he was that kind of guy.

Jeremiah walked along the shoulder of the road, kicking at clods of ice as he went. The light was fading fast; it was full dark a little after 5 P.M. at this time of year. The air was so cold that it hurt the insides of his nostrils, but the quiet was soothing. The rhythm of his steps lulled him into a quiet place, giving him the serenity that had escaped him at the funeral service. The smell of smoke carried on the air. This time of year, everyone around here supplemented their houses' heat with wood fires. The smell was heavy on the air today, which was unusual, because it was so clear and dry this evening.

Out of habit, he checked his parents' mailbox. Nothing, of course. He had already brought in the mail that afternoon—a pile of condolence cards and junk mail. He shut the mailbox's rusty door and walked past the thick evergreen trees that shrouded the end of the driveway. Once he was clear of the shrubbery, Jeremiah stopped. It wasn't a wood fire he smelled; it was a house fire. His parents' home—his home—stood engulfed in flames.

"No!" he cried, scrambling down the icy, rutted road. How could this happen in what was already the worst week of his life? He was glad he had kept his camera and his backpack with him, but everything else—every scrap of his life besides the few things he had taken to college—it was all vaporizing before his eyes. He heard sirens in the distance, which immediately took him back to his parents' accident. In shock, he watched the house burn.

Then he noticed he wasn't alone. A big, extended-cab pickup truck was parked near the bushes at the side of the property. He started toward it, but just then two men ran from the backyard and beat him to it. The driver jumped inside, gunned the engine, and put the truck in reverse, evidently aiming for Jeremiah, who ran back down the driveway, took a sharp right, and dove into the juniper bushes that flanked the mailbox.

The truck reached the bottom of the driveway. The driver rolled down the window and looked up and down the road for Jeremiah. He burrowed further into the junipers' spiny branches and waited, holding his breath.

"I don't see 'im anywhere. He must have had a car waiting for him. We'll find 'im." He rolled up his window and peeled out of the driveway, rushing south past Jeremiah's hiding place and into the night.

Jeremiah exhaled slowly. How long should he wait under cover? They could be back any second. He decided to sit tight until the fire trucks arrived.

Inexplicably, the red flag on the mailbox was now up. He'd checked it minutes ago. What was going on?

He skittered across the snow and opened the mailbox door. A large manila envelope had been stuffed inside. By whom? He grabbed it and hurried far back into the largest juniper bush.

He looked down at the envelope in his hands. What was it—the arsonists' calling card? He ripped it open and pulled out its contents. Among the pages was a piece of vellum.

"Adoption Certificate," it read at the top.

He scanned the page, his stomach dropping as he read.

He'd been adopted? Seriously? The joke he'd cracked in the minivan the day his parents died came back to him. They had known, but they'd chosen not to say anything. His real birth date was listed on the certificate, and the adoption was dated as effective his false birth date, December 7, 1990.

He rifled through the remaining sheets of paper to find more information. If Roger and Debra Whitney weren't his birth parents, who were? No other names were listed anywhere in the documentation.

Once again, Jeremiah's world was turned upside down. He heard a voice and flinched—were the arsonists returning? But it was only his video camera. It had dropped to the ground when he'd opened the envelope and was now playing back. The recording had rewound to the very beginning. Jeremiah picked it up and watched. He hadn't seen this early footage before.

It was his mother—or, Debra, he supposed—wrapping the camera up for his birthday. She was sitting in the minivan; Jeremiah wondered whether she had wrapped it in the parking lot of his dorm. She'd worked hard to get it running before she did so. "Are you sure we shouldn't have gotten him the printer?" she asked, doubt and excitement mingled in her voice.

Jeremiah heard his father's voice. "Honey, he's gonna love it."

"I know. I just want it recording when he opens it. To get his reaction. Want to say any words for the camera?"

Debra folded the wrapping paper back off the lens and held the camera up to frame Roger's face. He looked exasperated, but was clearly disarmed by his wife's charm. Jeremiah had seen similar exchanges between the two of them countless times over the years.

"Hi," he said with false brightness. "See you in five minutes!"

"Roger," she said. It was her turn to be exasperated. She set the camera face-up in its nest of wrapping paper.

"Happy birthday, Jeremiah," she cooed down into it. "We'll see you soon!"

Jeremiah watched, tears spilling out of his eyes as his mother covered the camera's lens with wrapping paper. He heard one last "Bye" from his father as the screen went black.

Jeremiah looked up at the stars, thick and bright in the winter sky. It hurt to see his parents again, so alive and normal, when just an hour ago, he had bid farewell to their bodies. Why was this happening to him? Who had left the information about his adoption in his mailbox—was it the same people who had just burned down his house? He didn't think life could possibly get any worse.

He looked down at the certificate again. It had to be a fake, planted to torture him, but why?

It seemed like the arsonists weren't coming back. Jeremiah crawled out of the bushes just as the first fire truck arrived. He followed it down the driveway. The blaze had already devoured the house by the time he had first gotten here. He knew that all the firefighters could do at this point was contain the blaze and try to keep it from spreading to anyone else's property. The police arrived soon after.

After the flames were out, the police took Jeremiah's statement and told him they'd file it with his parents' insurance company. This all felt sickeningly familiar. Jeremiah gave them the name and number of his parents' lawyer, glad that he had it with him.

"Can we take you somewhere—to a friend's house, or to a motel?" the fire chief asked.

Once again, Jeremiah couldn't face talking to anyone—not even Bishop Freeman. "Could you drop me off at the airport? I guess I'll just change my ticket and go back to college tomorrow morning."

"Sure thing," said the firefighter. "We'll call you if we discover anything that you need to know."

Jeremiah thought for a moment. Yes, leaving seemed like the best thing to do. He knew he'd be welcome to stay at the bishop's house, but what if the arsonists in the pickup found him there? He didn't want to bring any more trouble to the kind people here. He wanted to get back to Utah, where he could sort out all of this insanity.

At the airport, he called his grandparents to tell them what had happened. Shocked, they offered to pick him up at the Salt Lake City airport in the morning and drive him back to school. He declined, telling them he had already paid for the airport shuttle. They reluctantly agreed, but made him promise to call them the minute his final exams were over so that they could come get him.

Finals—right. He had to find some way to make it through them, and then he could collapse at Grandpa and Grandma Whitney's house and try to make sense of all that had happened. There had to be an explanation, and Jeremiah knew he wouldn't be able to rest—not truly—until he got to the bottom of what was going on.

With a bitter snort, he saw the silver lining: he wouldn't have to worry about a storage unit now. His dad had always joked that procrastination was the key to flexibility—there seemed to be some truth to that fake proverb after all.

In the airport's tiny lobby, he sat on a sculpted plastic chair that seemed designed to prevent sleep at any costs. His suit was likely ruined after sliding around in the snow and ice and bushes in it. At the very least, it was uncomfortably damp and horribly wrinkled. If she could see him, his Grandma Price would probably tell him he looked like a hobo, but that was the least of his worries.

He had to wait until morning for the next flight to Newark; there was nothing he could do now except wait. He settled down and tried to calm his frenzied mind. Should he buy a paperback and try to lose himself in its pages? Jeremiah doubted that he'd be able to concentrate enough to be able to read.

No, he'd attempt to rest. He scrounged up the happiest memory he had of his parents—hiking Bryce Canyon when he was thirteen. The summer had been hot, but the beauty of the red rocks against the cerulean sky captivated them all, and his normally preoccupied father relaxed and went with the flow in an unusual way. They hiked and laughed and talked, pointing out lizards and cactus blossoms. They kidded around and even had a food fight once—though they were careful to clean up the mess afterward.

Lost in memory and fatigue, he jumped when a shadow fell over him.

"Jeremiah?"

Re: Rice Krispie Treats 🏷 Inbox x

🖨 🔲

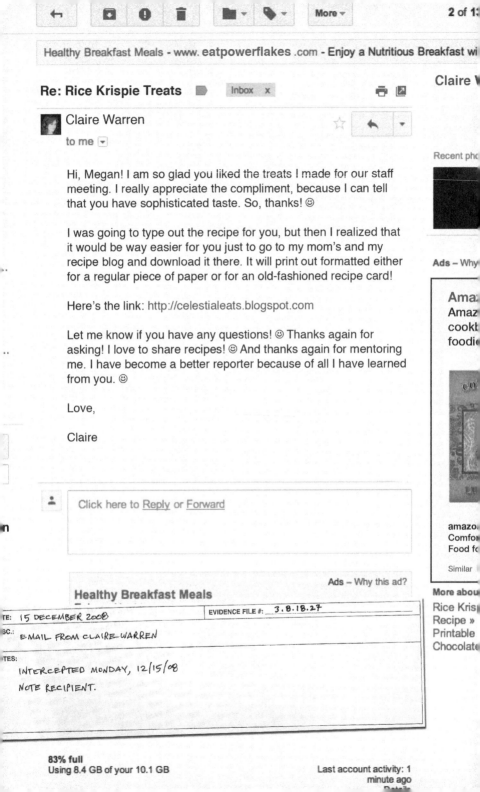

Claire Warren
to me ▾

Hi, Megan! I am so glad you liked the treats I made for our staff meeting. I really appreciate the compliment, because I can tell that you have sophisticated taste. So, thanks! ☺

I was going to type out the recipe for you, but then I realized that it would be way easier for you just to go to my mom's and my recipe blog and download it there. It will print out formatted either for a regular piece of paper or for an old-fashioned recipe card!

Here's the link: http://celestialeats.blogspot.com

Let me know if you have any questions! ☺ Thanks again for asking! I love to share recipes! ☺ And thanks again for mentoring me. I have become a better reporter because of all I have learned from you. ☺

Love,

Claire

Click here to Reply or Forward

Healthy Breakfast Meals

TE: 15 DECEMBER 2008   EVIDENCE FILE #: 3.8.18.27

SC.: EMAIL FROM CLAIRE WARREN

TES:

INTERCEPTED MONDAY, 12/15/08
NOTE RECIPIENT.

Claire W

Recent pho

More abou

Rice Kris
Recipe »
Printable
Chocolate

83% full
Using 8.4 GB of your 10.1 GB

Last account activity: 1
minute ago

CHAPTER SEVEN

Back to School

Bishop Freeman stood next to Jeremiah's seat in the airport lobby, a carry-on suitcase in his hand. Was he flying somewhere, too? Confused, Jeremiah sat up and rubbed his eyes. He had been closer to sleep than he had realized.

"Hey, Bishop," he said, sticking out his hand automatically. The bishop grasped it tightly, then let go. He sat down next to Jeremiah.

"I heard about the fire, but by the time I got there, you were gone." The bishop's tired, blue eyes crinkled into a sad smile. "I guess I understand why you'd want to get away from here as fast as possible, but people do care about you here, you know."

Jeremiah looked at his hands. "I'm sorry. I should've called you. You've done so much for us—me—already. You're right, though. I just . . ." His throat seized up.

The bishop wordlessly put his arm around Jeremiah and waited. After a couple of minutes, Jeremiah got his composure back.

"Sorry," he mumbled again.

"No need, son. No need." Bishop Freeman rolled the suitcase closer to Jeremiah. "After I saw what was left of your house, I went home and asked Karen to get a couple of Abel's old suits and some other clothes together for you. The way he's pumping iron on his off-days over in Afghanistan, I doubt these things will fit him once he finishes his tour. Anyway, I know you have stuff at college, but we thought this might help some, after all you've lost today."

Jeremiah hadn't ever heard the bishop utter so many words in a row outside of fast and testimony meeting before. Some snippet of misplaced pride tempted him to refuse the gift, but Jeremiah forced that down.

"That's so kind of you. I really appreciate it. Thanks. Please thank Sister Freeman—and Abel, whenever you talk to him next."

"Son . . ." Bishop Freeman paused. "I don't know if you know this, but your dad and I were missionary companions in England."

Jeremiah sat up. *Really?* He didn't remember his dad ever saying that. Of course, his father had never talked much about his mission, unlike a lot of Jeremiah's Young Men leaders, who tended to yammer on and on about their glory days.

The bishop went on. "You and I have known each other for only a few years—but I've known *about* you nearly your entire life. Your dad and I kept in touch after we both got home—a phone call or a Christmas card here or there—and when you moved to Seneca Falls, it was like a mission re-union for us. Your dad was one of the best, most spiritually sensitive missionaries I ever knew—and he got better with age. He was like a brother to me, and . . ." He stopped, head bowed, visibly wrestling with his emotions. His grip on Jeremiah's shoulder tightened.

"All that to say—you're like family to me. Keep in touch, if you can. You'll be in my prayers." The bishop drew Jeremiah into a long, tight hug, punctuated with several hard slaps on the back. After a few minutes, he drew away.

"Any way I can convince you to come home and catch a couple hours sleep in a real bed?"

Jeremiah smiled, but shook his head. "Thanks. This means so much—you don't know. I just . . . I'm worried about whoever set that fire. I don't want them following me to your house and causing more trouble."

The muscles in Bishop Freeman's jaw clenched and unclenched a few times. "Let them come," he said, staring off into space—and Jeremiah was suddenly glad that he was on the bishop's good side

"Oh. Karen sent this, too." The bishop pulled a large plastic container out of his coat pocket.

Jeremiah took it, certain that it contained far more food than he could eat in the next few hours. "Thanks," he said again.

"You're welcome, son. Listen, since I can't convince you to come home with me, I hope you don't mind if I stay and see you off."

Jeremiah, about to protest automatically, stopped and shut his mouth. He nodded. "It would be great to have your company, Bishop. Thanks."

• • •

Almost there.

Jeremiah gazed at the mountains out the window of the airport shuttle. They'd just passed the point of the mountain that marked the border of Salt Lake and Utah counties; he was just minutes from home. *Home.* The dorm was his only home now, unless you counted his grandparents' ranch in Manti. He wondered what he'd do when the school year was over in April. He already planned to spend the Christmas break in Manti—though Porter had offered to let him stay at his parents' house in Salt Lake. Maybe he'd split his time between the two. Would being with his grandparents bring up too many painful memories? Maybe, but the way he felt right now, he didn't know whether he could stand being around the relentlessly cheerful Porter Coolbrith and his family for days on end. Jeremiah sighed. He'd figure it out. Right now, he was just too tired.

Hours on planes would do that to you, even though you were just sitting in a chair doing nothing but flying through space at hundreds of miles per hour. He planned to sleep for as long as he could tomorrow. Then he'd get up, look over his notes for his Poli Sci final, and do his best on it.

His first semester had gone okay until last week. He'd gotten good grades so far, and he hoped that his performance in earlier weeks would make up for what would probably be pretty dismal results on his finals. Should he go to his professors and beg for extra time? Jeremiah hated the thought.

At such a big school, they must have heard every excuse in the book by now. No, he'd just suck it up and work his hardest and make up for it next semester. Winter semester would be the last before his mission. He'd make the most of it, then serve the Lord for two years. That had always been his plan.

He looked at the now grimy envelope in his hands. He'd gone over the adoption papers again, combing through the legalese for any hint as to his true parentage—or as to the papers' forgery—but had come up with nothing. Maybe Grandpa and Grandma Whitney could tell him more.

. . .

The shuttle pulled up to his dorm a few minutes later. Jeremiah grabbed his bags, got off, and walked up the sidewalk. Because he was looking at his feet, he didn't see anyone around him and jumped a little when he heard his name.

"Hey, Jeremiah. You're just in time! Could you get the door for me?"

Jeremiah turned and saw a pretty girl standing right next to him. How had he not heard her come up? She held a glass baking dish covered with plastic wrap, the sight of which made Jeremiah's stomach growl. He'd eaten Sister Freeman's ham sandwiches hours ago, and he suddenly realized that he was starving.

"Oh, yeah, sure. . . . Claire, right?" He recognized her now—the girl who had given him her sympathies in the cafeteria. Man, she was cute, those smiling brown eyes and soft, wavy hair framing her heart-shaped face. He felt his cheeks go hot and turned slightly so she wouldn't see him blush.

"Yeah," she said, and he could tell by her happy chirp that she was surprised he remembered her name. "Thank you," she said as he opened the door. She slipped under his arm and walked into the foyer.

"I hope the funeral was nice," she said timidly.

"It was fine." Jeremiah looked around the common room. Most of his ward seemed to be gathered there, some still in their Sunday clothes, some in pajamas. Was it some kind of party?

"So what exactly is going on here?" he asked.

"Ward prayer." Claire looked surprised; ward prayer was one of those routines, like FHE, that was well established at this point in the semester. Jeremiah pressed his lips together. *Of course.* He hadn't been sorry to miss church during his travels today, preferring to wallow a bit in a mire of self-pity than hear the messages of hope and deliverance that were a part of every talk during the month of December. After avoiding all that, he certainly didn't want to stand around here and explain himself over and over to well-meaning acquaintances.

"I just got in from New York," he started.

Claire smiled, understanding in her eyes. "Well, sometimes I don't feel like praying, either, but . . . we can use all the prayers we can get, right?"

Jeremiah knew she had a point, but he just couldn't take all these people right this minute. Looking at all of them milling around made him feel claustrophobic, and fatigue weighed on him heavily.

He sighed. "Right. Look, I just need to unpack, and I've got a lot to do before tomorrow, so . . ."

Claire apparently knew how to pick her battles. That was a refreshing change, and Jeremiah felt a rush of gratitude for her kindness as she said, "Take a treat with you before you go, then. I made them myself. My mom and I collect recipes together. Did you and your mom ever . . ." She trailed off, seeming to realize that this moment might not be the best to mention parents.

Jeremiah tried not to take it personally. She barely knew him and had no idea of even a tenth of what he'd been through lately. She was trying to make him feel better, and it wasn't her fault it hadn't worked. He tried for a smile as he took a Rice Krispie treat and a napkin from her then went up the back stairs.

In the stairwell, a kid he recognized from the third floor nearly barreled into him. "Hey, Jeremiah, you coming to ward prayer?"

"No!" he answered, more forcefully than he intended. Couldn't people mind their own business? Why should anyone care whether he showed up for some stupid group prayer that was really just an excuse to eat sugar and flirt?

He made it to the top of the stairs and fished his keys out of his pocket, then realized that his door was cracked open. Dang that Porter. He had to be more careful. He must be off somewhere with Lilah.

No. Something was wrong here. He sensed it even

before touching the door. Maybe he should leave again and go back to the safety of the group at ward prayer. No. He was exhausted. Would he ever get any rest? What was going to happen now—was his dorm going to burn down, too?

Hesitantly, he pushed the door open with effort; stuff littering the floor partially blocked it. Chaos. His lamp was on the floor, as were all of his books. Clothes lay everywhere, and posters had been half torn off the wall. His alarm clock blinked at him from the carpet, flashing zeros as if in distress.

A pair of long legs lay on the floor halfway out of his closet; as Jeremiah stuck his head farther in the door, he realized that they belonged to Simon. His arms and legs were tied up, and his mouth had a strip of duct tape over it. His eyes were closed, and his position on the floor looked awkward. Was he dead? Unconscious? Jeremiah felt a rush of relief when he looked more closely and saw that Simon was breathing.

Don't go in, a voice whispered.

That was ridiculous; he had to help his friend. Jeremiah mentally brushed aside the warning and stepped into his room to untie Simon. Maybe his goofy neighbor had seen something, but Jeremiah had to get him freed and conscious before he could find out anything about who had done this.

He stepped into the room and felt one last flash of warning just as a hand grabbed his shoulder. He whirled and looked into the face of a tall man with a flashing blue earpiece stuck to the side of his head like a barnacle.

As the man drew him close with a sneer, Jeremiah heard a tinny voice coming through the high-tech earpiece.

"Magus? Magus, what's going on?"

Magus? What did that mean—was it some kind of code? Or was it his attacker's name? It must be the latter. Terrified, Jeremiah twisted out of the man's grasp. He dropped his backpack and the envelope containing his adoption papers onto the floor and stumbled out of his room. Not looking backward, he fairly flew down the hall and down the stairs.

His parents had been killed before his eyes. His house had been torched, and now his dorm room had been violated—and he had been powerless throughout. What did he have left? Who was it that was bent on ruining his life, systematically, and with seemingly unlimited power and resources? And how could he—alone and not knowing his enemy—possibly fight back?

ChObO: ck Out
H#166: m3t3r
xl4t3s into
b1n4ry! WOOt!
LOL

3:14 PM

CHAPTER EIGHT

Abide with Me

Jeremiah heard Magus—if that was his name—catching up to him as he took the back staircase of the dorm two stairs at a time. He ran out the door and into the street, not knowing where to go to elude his pursuer. His mind exhausted, he let his body take him where it would. He ran past the women's dorms and crossed the street toward the complex of classroom buildings.

Should he go to one of the blue help boxes and pull the alarm? What good would that do? Whoever was chasing him had gotten past dorm security, trashed his room, and tied up his friend—all with no one the wiser. He doubted that campus rent-a-cops would be any help.

He heard voices raised in the harmony of a hymn and ran toward them. Entering the lit tunnel that connected the football stadium's parking lot to the rest of campus, he passed a group of tunnel singers. They were good, he noted absently. Not all tunnel singers were created equal, he had discovered in his short time at college.

Lungs bursting, he ran toward the parking garage outside

the stadium. He had to rest; maybe he could hide there long enough to catch his breath and figure out a plan. He ran up the second level and past several rows of cars.

• • •

Porter passed by the kids gathered for ward prayer, not lured at all by the sight of diverse refreshments. Lilah had made him some penuche fudge with pecans, and he was as full as a tick. "Stuffed like a blood sausage," as Grandpa Rockwell had been fond of saying. *Heh.*

Porter looked forward to crashing long and hard and avoiding the thought of his American History final for as long as possible. Lilah had helped him study, and he felt prepared, but Porter hated taking tests like poison, and all his work might be for naught if he didn't get a decent night's sleep.

When would Jeremiah be back from Seneca Falls? Poor guy. Porter walked down the hall toward his room, noting that the door was ajar. Jeremiah must have gotten home already, but why would he leave the door open? That wasn't like him; he was always such a neat freak, and growing up in the East had apparently made him paranoid about locking doors, too. Porter pushed the door farther open, forcing it past blankets and other stuff that littered the floor.

"What in the J. Golden Kimball?" he muttered, then caught sight of Simon on the carpet.

Blast that kid and his over-the-top Live Action Role-Playing games. Why did the mayhem have to spread to

Porter's room? Porter had bonded with Simon early in the semester over their shared interest in LARPs. But Simon's group of elf wannabes, *The Summer Islanders,* was getting out of hand. Porter had to try to convince Simon to switch to the *Medievalists.* They had way cooler weapons and a much better sense of propriety and boundaries. It was Sunday, for the love of Moroni.

He knelt by Simon's side and ripped the duct tape off his mouth, which had the bonus effect of restoring Simon to consciousness.

"Dark Elves!" the kid exclaimed, staring off into space.

I knew it. "Look," Porter said. "This whole role-playing thing of yours has gone too far."

"Retaliation by the losing guild," Simon explained, as if Porter could keep all of his hijinks straight. "The Dark Elves lost the last invasion, but now they've gone too far."

Porter pondered that, but it didn't sit right with him. He looked around the room. It was utterly trashed—as if someone had been looking for something, then gotten furious when they didn't find it. "The nerd brigade did this?"

Brian popped his head in the door. *Of course.* The guy had an instinct for trouble. He should apply for a job at Zooby News. He'd fit in well there.

"What are you doing?" Brian asked, and Porter couldn't restrain the sarcasm. He was glad Lilah wasn't there to get on his case about it.

"I'm getting my knot-tying merit badge," he said with fake sincerity. "Wanna help?" He rolled his eyes. "The Uruk-Hai came in and attacked Simon."

Brian looked around the room, clearly skeptical. "Simon's friends did this?" He picked a backpack off the floor.

Aha, so Jeremiah *had* returned. Weird that he'd drop his stuff and leave, though. A framed photo lay on the carpet next to the backpack, the glass shattered and the frame bent. Jeremiah's parents.

Oh, no. Porter's whole body zinged with adrenaline-fueled alarm. "Where's Jeremiah?" He didn't expect an answer.

Brian shrugged. Porter jumped up and pushed past him and out of the room.

As he ran down the hall, Brian called after him. "Porter!"

Porter paused and turned. "Simon's friends didn't do this. Call the cops."

Brian looked at him in confusion. "Where are you going?"

Crap. He was only halfway down the hall and already out of breath. He had to get back into shape soon. That awesome fudge was now starting to feel like a lead weight in his stomach. Wheezing, he stopped for a moment. "I don't know," he said, and started running again.

Please help me find him, Heavenly Father, he prayed as he ran. *Please help me not to have a heart attack on the way.*

Miraculously, he felt energy course through him. Was it the Spirit or the sugar? Or was the Spirit using the sugar? Did it even matter? Suddenly, he knew which way to go, as if Jeremiah had left a trail behind him as he escaped—what? Who was chasing him?

Porter would find out soon enough. He followed Jeremiah's trail as if it were lit up by neon.

.   .   .

Jeremiah crouched behind the back tire of a parked car, trying to keep his breathing quiet even as his lungs ached for extra oxygen. He heard footsteps, slow but determined, echoing on the concrete. His pursuer was nearly on top of him. Jeremiah angled his head to scope out the scene using the car's side mirror; the coast looked clear. He scooted sideways, carefully lifting his feet so his sneakers wouldn't squeak, hoping to get around the car and maybe hide under the front.

The parking garage was freezing, but the cold was the least of his worries as he slowly levered himself toward the car's front end.

Suddenly, someone caught him from behind and jerked him upright. Magus was about Jeremiah's height, but had the advantage of at least twenty pounds of muscle on him. He was fantastically strong, slamming Jeremiah's head into the wall and holding him there.

"Where's the box?" Magus snarled.

The box? Was that what this was all about? Jeremiah hadn't seen the box—had pushed away guilty thoughts about it—ever since that awful night at the gas station. What had happened to it? He had assumed it had been stolen when he had dropped it trying to rescue his parents. He had no idea where it was now, and he didn't really care. Magus squeezed

Jeremiah's windpipe as if trying to choke an answer out of him.

"I don't know," Jeremiah sputtered, gasping for a breath around the claw that was inexorably closing off his throat.

Magus shook him, sending another spasm of pain through his windpipe. "You don't *know,* or you won't *say? Where is the box?*"

Jeremiah gazed into the eyes of his attacker.

He sounds English, Jeremiah noted through his disorientation.

Magus looked familiar somehow. Had Jeremiah met him before? The man shook him again, and Jeremiah's focus snapped back. "I lost it," he blurted out, shame welling up inside him and breaking through his defiant apathy over the whole incident.

If being entrusted with that box had been the start of all of the awful things that had happened, then they had all been in vain. The box was gone.

As if he could read Jeremiah's thoughts, Magus whispered, "You are the reason your parents are dead."

The taunt confirmed Jeremiah's worst fears, and despair began to darken his mind. He closed his eyes and mumbled a desperate prayer.

Magus cackled. "Are you talking to your god? He can't hear you." He pressed his gloved hand against Jeremiah's forehead, forcing his eyes open. "You're a failure." He grinned, clearly enjoying the effect of his malicious words. He went on. "Had you not pulled over at that gas station in Manti, they might still be alive."

Jeremiah's eyes welled with tears. The emotional tor-
ment was far worse than the physical pain. He tried to twist
free of Magus's grasp, but his attacker had him pinned.

"Even if God does exist, it doesn't seem like He's doing
much to take care of you." Magus smiled again, seeming to
draw energy from Jeremiah's pain.

Suddenly, the pressure was off Jeremiah's throat. He
fell hard to the frozen concrete and drew in a huge gulp of
air, but choked on it. His trachea was already swelling. He
looked up as he coughed. Porter had appeared out of nowhere and must have hauled Magus off of him. With a roar,
Porter whacked the guy on the back of the head. Magus
slumped to the cold ground, unconscious. Porter stood over
the man, eyes wide and chest heaving, as if amazed at his
own strength. Not pausing to gloat, he rushed to Jeremiah
and yanked him up by his arm.

"Come on," he urged. After a few steps, they both
looked back to make sure the man hadn't awakened.

He had vanished. Jeremiah looked at Porter in confusion and fear. Porter shook his head and shrugged, and they
limped together out of the parking garage.

Outside, Jeremiah could hear the tunnel singers once
more. They'd switched to "Joy to the World," and with a sad
jolt, Jeremiah realized that Christmas was just a few days
away. Would he ever feel the joy of this season again? He
and Porter stood for a moment, watching snow swirl down.

Porter looked around as if searching for more mysterious attackers, then half supported, half dragged Jeremiah
across the sidewalk and up a snowy slope studded with trees

and bushes. They sat down in the snow, and Porter handed Jeremiah's camera case to him. Jeremiah took it more eagerly than he should have. He couldn't believe he'd dropped it somewhere along the way to the parking garage. But maybe it had helped Porter find him.

Porter stared at him for a few moments, still getting his breath back. Sweat steamed off him in the bitterly cold air. Finally he said, "I think I have a right to know why a British guy dressed in black is trying to kill my roommate." He waited, expectation on his face. When Jeremiah didn't answer, he pressed, "What box did he want?"

Jeremiah searched his soul. How could he explain this? He'd promised not to talk about the box. He had to keep at least one of the trusts he'd been given on his false birthday. He shook his head.

"We're not going anywhere until you tell me," Porter warned.

Jeremiah swallowed and looked away. "I . . . I can't."

"You mean you won't."

Jeremiah hated the way Porter's wounded words echoed those of his attacker. He turned to his roommate, who had probably just saved his life, and who deserved better treatment. "No, I can't. I promised."

Porter mulled this over and finally nodded. He rested a meaty hand on Jeremiah's back. "You know, Grandpa Rockwell shot a man between the eyes once just for looking at Joseph Smith wrong. I'll do the same for you." He looked at Jeremiah again, who wondered for the hundredth time how his roommate's mood always bounced back to its default cheerfulness. "Come on, let's go."

Warmth spread through Jeremiah's chest, even as his backside froze on the snowy slope. "Wait . . . wait." He closed his eyes for a second, listening. Should he confide in Porter?

Yes, the warmth assured him. *You can trust him with this now.*

"I think . . . I feel like I'm supposed to tell you."

Porter stared at him. "You think? Or you know?"

The warmth suffused throughout Jeremiah now, his ears throbbing almost painfully with it. "I know."

Below them, the tunnel singers started "Abide with Me." Jeremiah closed his eyes against the sudden pain that knifed through his heart. Sister Jepson had sung that at his parents' funeral. He blinked back tears. Would he ever be able to hear that hymn again without crying? Porter sat down next to him, his bearlike bulk a shield from the cold wind. Jeremiah took a deep breath and started talking.

• • •

From the parking garage, a white-haired man wearing a long, denim coat and yellow work gloves watched the pair huddled on the frozen hillside. After a few moments, he turned away, satisfied that Jeremiah was safe.

31 St. Alphonsus Road
Clapham, U.K. SW4 0AA

Dear Mom and Dad,

DATE: 10 JULY 1983
DESC.: R. WHITNEY LETTER
EVIDENCE FILE #: 4.4.4
NOTES: AIRMAIL LETTER FROM ELDER ROGER WHITNEY TO HIS PARENTS
DATED 10 JULY 1983.
IS LOUVAIN MORRIS THE HISTORIAN AND ANCIENT DOCUMENTS EXPER

Happy Independence Day! I'm a little late, I know, but it's obviously not a holiday they mention much here in Merrie Olde England, so I kind of forgot about it. I hope your Fourth was ripping (which means "awesome"). Did you watch the fireworks from Temple Hill? Did Marilyn's annoying boyfriend show up? I can just taste the hot dogs and Mom's potato salad as I write.

I just transferred here yesterday, and my new comp Elder Thomas and I are backed up on laundry, so I have to write fast. Priorities, right, Mom? But I do want to tell you about the miraculous baptism I was privileged to perform this last week.

I don't know if you remember me telling you a couple of months ago about when Elder Freeman and I tracted out this crazy girl up in Islington. She's the one who called us "crass Americans,"—which was rich coming from a pregnant, homeless-looking chick with a mohawk and a face full of piercings—then shut the door in our faces and caught my favorite purple tie in her greasy latch. Yeah, I tried to get the stain out with dish soap, but that just made it worse, so I had to chuck it. If you ever see another one like it when you're at the mall, Mom, I'd love it if you could send it to me. That tie rocked.

Even though it was a terrible end to a terrible day, the punk girl kept coming back to my mind during comp prayer

1

about our investigators. I didn't know how I'd get the guts to go back to her house.

Anyway, we ran into her a couple of weeks later in the Islington High Street, and she was like a changed person. She came right up to us, smiled, and said hello. (Most people avoid our eyes when we're out, like they think we're going to kidnap them and brainwash them, or something.) And the Spirit hit me harder than it has during my whole entire mission: she was going to get baptized. Quickly. And that after that, she'd be in terrible danger.

I reeled a bit, but fortunately, Elder Freeman picked up the slack, bless his little green heart. He reintroduced us and found out her first name. (Which is another one for the wacky British file, by the way: Louvain. Although I guess it's actually a French name. Whatever. Her last name is Morris, so that's at least normal.)

So while I was having the Spirit knock me over the head about the woman standing right in front of us, Freeman made an appointment to teach her the first discussion that very night. She said she'd had a dream about us and wanted to tell us about it. That made me a little nervous, because I thought she might be hitting on us. But she's already pregnant, so I decided it shouldn't be a problem.

So, yeah, we met at the park and taught her that evening, and she turned out to be the most golden investigator of all time. (She and her boyfriend broke up right after she found out about the baby, so she's on her own for now.) She asked all the right questions and none of the wrong ones, and the Spirit was thick around us. She felt it too, and her

2

countenance started to change even more—right before our eyes. Alma 5:19, and all. If I hadn't had that revelation earlier that day, I would have thought she was scamming us.

But, no—she kept right on lapping up the gospel like it was the sweetest water in the world—and I baptized her last Sunday. The whole branch showed up—it was an awesome service. I've enclosed some photos we ran through the FotoRush place so that we could give her copies before transfer day. It was about the greatest day of my life.

I still have a sense that she is in danger though. I wanted to tell her about that, but she was in this happy bubble, and I didn't want to burst that. I'll definitely keep in touch with her after my mission, though of course I can't write to her while I'm here.

Actually, Mom, would you mind dropping her a line? I know that the sisters who transferred into our area will take good care of her but Louvain needs to stay close. I don't know why I have this feeling about her but I do. She's going to need help.

I wrote her address on the back of the photo of her and me and Freeman outside the chapel. Please write to her and—I don't know—bear your testimony or something. Just keep in touch with her until I get home. It's important.

Criminy, this has gotten way too long. Thomas and I have got to get to the launderette. Stay close to the Lord, Mom and Dad! I know you will.

Love from your son,

Elder Whitney

CHAPTER NINE

Lineage

It was a typical, bitterly cold January day—but at least the sun was shining. His arms overly full, Jeremiah struggled along the sidewalk. Why had he tried to bring everything into the dorm in one trip? He was almost to the porch, if he could just keep from spilling his clean, folded laundry all over the snow. Grandma Whitney had insisted on doing it, and all his clothes looked and smelled far better than they had in months. He didn't want to undo all of that industry in one fell swoop.

"Hey, Jeremiah," the quiet kid from down the hall called out. Jeremiah couldn't remember his name. Oh, right: Tyler. Or was it Taylor? "Where'd you go for break?"

Jeremiah didn't remember Tyler/Taylor speaking in anything but a mumble all last semester. What had transformed him into a smiling person voluntarily calling out greetings? Jeremiah peeked around his paired socks. *Aha.* He was walking with a girl. Good for him. Love was rumored to bring you out of your shell like that. Excellent.

"Oh, hey," Jeremiah answered. "I went . . . uh, I stayed with Porter."

He'd remembered in the nick of time that he didn't want any more attention drawn to his family in Manti. He and Porter had decided that staying over Christmas break at the Coolbrith home in Salt Lake would be Jeremiah's cover story. Tyler/Taylor nodded happily and looked at the girl, apparently satisfied.

Carefully balancing his laundry basket on his forearm, he swung open the door to the dorm and started up the stairs.

After puffing up to the landing two flights of stairs later, Jeremiah stopped outside his door. It was open. That was normal he reminded himself, ignoring his flashback to the chase in the parking garage weeks before. He pushed the door open a little farther. Porter had arrived early. That was unusual. Maybe he had made some New Year's resolutions or something.

Jeremiah stopped, stricken as he gazed around at the walls of their room. It looked like a party supply store had exploded inside. Pink and purple crepe paper streamers festooned the walls, interspersed with cheerful quotes written on construction paper in magic marker.

"What happened here?"

Porter looked up from the giant armchair, which he was wrestling into an upright position. "Oh!" he said, glancing at the lavish decorations. "It's Lilah's Christmas present. She thought that the bad guys would leave us alone if it looked like a girl's apartment in here." He patted his dilapidated piece of furniture lovingly.

"She put this in the dumpster."

Wow. Jeremiah was impressed. That chair had to weigh three times as much as Lilah.

He watched Porter struggle to lift it again. "I don't even know how the heck she got it in there. But this is a man's room, and it needs a man's chair." Finally, he heaved the chair into position and collapsed on top of it.

Jeremiah put his laundry away, then took a framed photo of his parents out of the bottom of the basket and set it on the headboard of his bed. He stared down at it for a moment. It had been five weeks since they'd been killed, and the pain when he thought of them was still as fresh and raw as it had been on his birthday. His *fake* birthday, he amended— though he could see why his parents had chosen it, since it was the day he was adopted. But why the subterfuge? Why did he need to have a different birthday? Even after the things he discovered over Christmas break, he still had so many questions.

As if reading his mind, Porter asked, "So, do you ever wonder who your real parents are?"

"The adoption papers have to be fake," Jeremiah said, though he didn't really believe that. Admitting that they could be real implied that he might have to start looking for birth parents—who had rejected him in the first place. No, his *real* parents were the people who had raised him.

Porter cleared his throat, and Jeremiah turned to look at him with dread. Porter only made that noise when he was about to say something unpleasant. "Yeah. I might have had

Lilah's grandma verify them with the New York Adoption Registry."

Jeremiah glared at Porter, his mouth open in amazement. Porter held up his hands to forestall an attack. "She works at the Family History Center. And, I dunno, whoever stuffed your adoption papers in your mailbox probably had a reason. Shouldn't you find out why?"

"And they burned down my house for a reason."

Porter shook his head. "Maybe the same person who gave you the box wants you to find your real parents."

"My real parents are buried in Seneca Falls." He looked at Porter, still angry at his betrayal. "I just can't believe you told Lilah's grandma." He started unpacking his luggage, swallowing the lump in his throat and trying not to cry. Not now. Not in front of Porter.

"Your secret's safe," Porter said, clearly realizing he had crossed a line. "Come on, Jay. Let's go down to the Family History Center and we'll talk to Lilah's grandma. She totally loves me."

• • •

Next door, Brian sat on his bed, listening to his neighbors' conversation with a government-issue surveillance device. He had bought it for cheap at a flea market back home in Santa Clara, and it was proving to be worth its weight in gold. He scribbled furiously, attempting to transcribe their words. Exactness was important in these cases; there was no telling when what seemed to be a casual turn of phrase was actually code.

•   •   •

Jeremiah and Porter walked into their Old Testament class. Porter had coaxed Jeremiah into taking it, and Jeremiah had agreed, even though he feared that his roommate would merely be a homework parasite, and not the "study buddy" he promised to be.

Porter brought up the stupid Family History Center again. Why was he so unwilling to let it go? Why couldn't he just admit that he'd been wrong in taking Lilah's grandmother into his confidence? With Jeremiah's luck, his past would be all over the Relief Society network in no time.

"What are you afraid of?" Porter asked, nudging Jeremiah in the ribs. "It's the Family History Center. It's just micro-fishies and old ladies. What could happen?"

Jeremiah sat down, and Porter flopped onto the chair next to him. "Look," Jeremiah said in an undertone. "You can tell me all about it when you get back. I'm not going." He looked around carefully. The class was filling with students as the professor was fiddling with a projector. Jeremiah couldn't be too careful; he never knew who might be listening.

•   •   •

Megan Halling walked up the back steps of the men's freshman dorm cautiously. She wasn't supposed to be in this part of the building, and she couldn't afford to be put on academic probation—not at this stage of her career. She had already accumulated a couple of warnings in her file, so she had to tread carefully. She looked up and down the hall of the third floor before entering to make sure she was alone. All was quiet. Working quickly, she went to Jeremiah's door, knelt, and began picking the lock with two hairpins. The YouTube video had made it look relatively simple, and she'd practiced for quite a while on her own door. It should just take a second—

A sword slid under her nose—bright, shiny steel, and it looked sharp.

"Declare your allegiance," came a voice from behind.

"What?" she said. *Who on earth?*

Whoever it was standing behind her bent close enough that she could feel his breath on her neck. As he spoke, she smelled Twizzlers, which reminded her of her dad. Red licorice was his favorite junk food. "Listen," the person holding the sword murmured. "You tell Tom and the rest of the Dark Elves to keep the battle out of the dorms. One break-in was enough."

Megan slowly turned her head. This wasn't some crazy black-ops guy; he looked like a normal, gangly freshman— as long as you expanded your definition of "normal" to include the knowledge of how to hold a broadsword properly.

"Break-in?" she asked, intrigued. The guy with the sword obviously lived on this floor; he must know Jeremiah at least slightly. The break-in he mentioned couldn't have been a theft, since freshmen didn't have anything worth stealing. Was someone else trying to find out more about the mysterious Jeremiah?

"Don't play ignorant," the guy said. He was cute, in a baby seal sort of way—curly red hair almost long enough to violate the grooming code, round blue eyes. Because of the Twizzler breath and the hair, she mentally dubbed him "Red Elf." Megan usually preferred her men tall, dark, and morose, but this one looked fresh—acceptable for use as a palate cleanser.

Red Elf continued, his eyes getting even wider as if he realized something. "You're not part of the Dark Elves, are you." It wasn't a question. Megan decided to fess up—sort of. She turned on the charm.

"No, I'm Megan Halling. Zooby News. I'm doing a story on your friend Jeremiah, and he sent me back to get his camera. But he forgot to give me the key. You wouldn't happen to have a spare, would you?"

Red stared at her, his mouth hanging open in a vacuous smile. Her act worked every time; it was almost like a superpower. He shook his head, apparently only now realizing that she'd asked him a question. A head poked out from behind the next door down. Some slightly greasy, Spooky Mulder type—also not Megan's preferred breed.

"You're not going to find the camera." Spooky spoke with conviction. This one might be worth talking to, unlike Red Elf, with his trusty sword. "He never lets it out of his sight." Spooky frowned at her. She had to be careful; he looked smart—and he'd clearly been listening to her conversation with Red, which meant that he was suspicious as well. "What do you want to know about Jeremiah, anyway? I don't think he sent you."

Megan smiled. He might be smarter than Red, but there were few men that she couldn't sway once she turned the full force of her persuasive abilities on them. Down the hall, a door slammed, and Megan looked around, flinching. She could *not* afford to get caught up here. She glanced at Spooky, who was unmoved.

Red bounced on the balls of his feet nervously. "Maybe we'd better let her in, in case somebody sees us with her."

Spooky squinted and pursed his lips like an old woman. Did he have something to hide? Megan's interest was aroused even further. Finally, he made a decision.

"Avert your eyes from the walls," he warned as he ushered her into his dorm room. Red followed. As Megan disregarded Spooky's instructions and looked at the walls, she realized that Red must be Spooky's roommate. One half of the room was decorated in full Tolkien regalia, while the other half—what *was* this? Posters, handbills, photographs, all scrawled on with magic marker and connected by red strings held in place with pushpins. Conspiracy theorist in prep-school garb? Spooky might be more interesting than he looked. Hidden depths.

Spooky saw her scanning his walls and got in her face. "I mean it. Girls are not supposed to be in here, and I have no problem reporting you to the Honor Code Office."

Red cut in. "No he won't." He seemed like he was trying to reassure her out of a sense of chivalry. "He's practically on probation after—"

Spooky slugged Red in the arm. "Do you want me to tell her about Wuggie?"

Red shut up immediately, glaring at his roommate. Spooky glared back. Megan decided to regain control of the situation. She focused on Spooky, since he looked to be the more valuable of the two.

"So, I was looking at your walls. I can see that you follow Dr. Calbert Davenport, too. . . ." She let her voice trail off, hoping he'd take the bait.

Spooky looked from her to Red. *Bingo.* He knew something; he was making the connections that she'd been assigned to make. He could help her. She turned the charisma up a notch.

"You don't have to say," she said in her sexiest whisper. "You never know who could be listening." She sidled a little closer to Spooky. "That's the main reason I'm a reporter—to expose the truth. Like Davenport."

Spooky was speechless. Fabulous. She had him practically hypnotized.

"Yeah," he said. Perfect. Inarticulateness from someone who probably usually couldn't shut up. Megan pressed on, improvising as she went.

"That's actually why I'm here. I came to investigate whether there is any connection to Professor Davenport's disappearance and the break-in in Jeremiah's room. I thought if I . . . *we* . . . could look at the footage on Jeremiah's video camera . . ." She trailed off suggestively.

Spooky looked at her for a moment. She could almost see the cogs of his clever little mind whirling away. "We don't have keys, and it's pretty much impossible to get duplicates made."

Lame. She'd thought he could do better than that. Forget it. She had to get out of here and cut her losses before she got caught.

"But I do have some other information," Spooky said as she reached for the doorknob. His voice held desperation; maybe he could be useful after all. "This may be helpful," he said, going to his wall and peeling back a poster of the Loch Ness Monster. Taped to the back of it was a manila envelope.

• • •

Jeremiah sat up as the professor cleared his throat and began speaking. "Welcome, everybody. This is Religion 301: Doctrines of the Old Testament. So if you thought you were in some Marriage Preparation class, you're in the wrong room." That got a few courtesy laughs, which intensified as a couple got up, packed up their notebooks, and left quickly.

"After the prayer, I'd like to address the topic of lineage. Any volunteers?"

Next to Jeremiah, Porter scooted downward in his seat until the back of his head was leaning on the desk behind him. He closed his eyes. He had the amazing talent of being able to nap anywhere.

Jeremiah elbowed him. "It's the first day, and you're already sleeping through class?"

Porter put his feet up and didn't answer. Jeremiah pulled out his notebook and a pen. His roommate leaned over. "Oh, Jay, mark attendance for me when the roll comes around." He closed his eyes again and settled back.

Jeremiah had never really gotten the point of most of the Old Testament, not even when his mother had taught it in seminary. It had always seemed pretty R-rated, actually—an awful lot of sex and violence. But he'd had a strong prompting that he should take this class, and he planned on paying attention. He uncapped his pen and sat forward, listening intently.

• • •

Spooky laid several documents out across the bed in precise rows. "This points to the fact that an even larger organization may be involved," he finished. Megan had barely managed to follow him through his labyrinth of paranoia, but she could see seeds of truth in what he'd put together. Maybe Davenport was more than a conspiracy-addicted nut job, after all.

Suddenly Red Elf darted forward and picked something up out of Spooky's stack. It looked like a photo of an official document. He read it and gasped. "Jeremiah's adopted?" he said incredulously.

Megan snatched the photo out of Red's hands and read it for herself. "Where did you get this?" she asked Spooky.

He backed up under the intensity of her gaze. "I . . . acquired it. I could get more."

Triumph flooded through Megan. This was working out after all. She was that much closer to helping her dad *and* proving herself to her mentor. "You would do that for me?" She leaned close and batted her eyelashes ever so slightly. *Bam.* She had him back. Time to retreat. "You know what? I just realized something. I'm a girl," she said, touching her sternum lightly. "And you're boys. And I'm not supposed to be here."

"Except every other Sunday from 3:00 to 8:00," supplied Red helpfully. Megan ignored him and smiled at Spooky again. She fished inside her purse.

"Here's my card. Let me know if you find anything else, huh?"

Spooky looked like he was at a loss for words. He seemed to be searching for something to keep her attention. Men were absurdly easy to read. How did they not realize it?

"Has Jeremiah told you about the box?" he blurted out.

Megan waited, intrigued again.

"I heard him and Porter talking about it this morning."

Was that it? A box? Her impatient sarcasm must have shown on her face, because he scrambled again. "I could find out some more intel."

"Do," Megan commanded sweetly. "Talk to you later." She wiggled her fingers coquettishly. These two were completely in her thrall. It was an excellent feeling. She would enjoy toying with them another time. She'd have to research their names, now that she thought of it. They hadn't indulged in that particular social nicety during their time together.

Megan clicked the earpiece of her phone as she left the

men's dorm. Brenna, her supervisor at zoobynews.com, was on speed dial. As always, she picked up on the first ring.

"Hello?"

Megan didn't bother saying hello. That was one of the things she appreciated about her mentor: even though Brenna was hugely pregnant at the moment, she was all business, all the time. So Megan cut to the chase. "Did you know he was adopted?"

"Just a minute." Brenna said nothing for several seconds; it sounded like she was moving to a quieter spot in the chaotic newsroom. Megan heard the gentle thud of a door being closed. "Are you absolutely certain?"

Megan smiled. "I have a photo of the adoption certificate," she said with triumph. Brenna didn't respond. Wasn't this the coup Megan thought it was?

"Is that it?"

Megan scrambled. She'd interrupted Brenna and hadn't delivered enough to make it worth the breach of etiquette. "He said something about a box."

That changed everything. Megan could almost feel Brenna's enthusiasm pouring through the phone. "Did you see it?"

Taken aback, Megan replied, "No."

"Find that box, and your career is made." Brenna clicked off the connection without a good-bye, as brusque as usual.

Megan did a silent fist-pump. Her instincts had served her well—the last piece of information retrieved was always the most valuable. That box had to be why Brenna and her superiors were so interested in Jeremiah. Megan decided that she was the one who would find it. Maybe she should cozy up to Claire, who was obviously carrying a torch for the boy. She walked toward her car, planning her next move.

• • •

Jeremiah elbowed Porter. If his roommate was going to snore the whole time, Jeremiah would sit somewhere else during the next class. He listened carefully as the professor spoke.

"Each of the twelve sons of Israel received unique blessings from their father. Where we come from matters. Our lineage matters."

Jeremiah felt the truth of that sink into his heart. Maybe he needed to research the circumstances of his adoption after all.

"Now, even if we're not born in the covenant, when we're baptized, we are adopted into the house of Israel," continued the professor. "Thus we gain certain blessings from both our birth family, as well as from our adopted family."

Whoa. Jeremiah knew that the professor was speaking figuratively, but the literal truth hit him hard. He put his pen down; he had the feeling that he'd remember every word of this lecture even without his notes. What was this feeling welling up inside him? He pondered it even as he kept listening. Miraculously, Porter was now wide awake. That had to be a sign in and of itself.

He reached over and poked Jeremiah in the ribs. "You

listening to this?" he said, not quite sotto voce. Jeremiah waved him quiet; he didn't want to miss a word.

"Ultimately when you look at your lineage and ask who you are, the most important lineage to know is that you are a child of God. You therefore have the potential to become as He is and inherit everything He has."

Jeremiah fought back tears. The professor was right. Jeremiah had to stop wallowing in grief and despair over what had happened to his parents. Even if he hadn't been born to Roger and Debra Whitney, so much of what he was had come from them. They had raised him and loved them. Even though he had inherited traits from his birth parents, he would always be a Whitney. But the first step toward sorting all this out was finding out who his birth parents were. He had to get to the Family History Center as soon as possible.

He glanced at Porter. He looked like such a buffoon sometimes, but his gruff exterior concealed a big heart and a fair amount of wisdom. He had done the right thing when he mentioned Jeremiah's circumstances to Lilah's grandmother. Jeremiah just hoped she wasn't the kind of chatty old lady who'd let the details of his background drop casually—for her safety as well as his own.

Jeremiah remembered his house engulfed in flames, almost every tangible piece of evidence of his first eighteen years vaporized before his eyes. He had to arise from the ashes and start his life over.

A strange thought occurred to him. Why had his parents bought a cemetery plot in Seneca Falls? They'd lived there for three years. They had moved a lot throughout Jeremiah's childhood, and had never put down roots like that before. Roger and Debra both grew up in Manti; why wouldn't they have wanted to be buried there, where generations of their families had been put to rest? His grandparents hadn't brought up the oddity either.

Jeremiah never thought that his parents would stay in Seneca Falls; he'd assumed his dad's job would transfer them yet again—maybe to Texas or Nebraska. What had made them buy that plot? Had they known that they were going to die?

Jeremiah wished he had something to go on. His father's missionary journals—stored in his grandparents' basement—had given him a lot of insight into the man his father was when he was Jeremiah's age. But those journals were more than twenty years old. He wished again that he had some later record of his father's spiritual thoughts and impressions.

He decided to go home and reread all the letters his parents had written him over the first four months of college. He was glad he'd saved them, following yet another seemingly unimportant impression. They were nearly all that remained of his parents. And maybe they held a clue to the situation Jeremiah found himself in now. Maybe there were references that he hadn't recognized on first reading them, but that would make sense if he looked at them again, given everything that had happened in the past month.

After the closing prayer, he gathered up his things and practically ran out the door. Porter was hard on his heels.

"Whoa, there, cowboy. Where are you off to in such a hurry?"

"I've got to get back to our room," Jeremiah said. "I've got to find something. Oh, and hey—you were right. I'm sorry. I need to go to the Family History Center and see Lilah's grandmother. Can you ask her what time would be best? Hopefully we can go tonight."

Porter grinned. "I was *right.* Where's your video camera? I want to preserve this moment. It's nice to hear you say those words. I hope I hear them more often in the future." He savored that for a moment. "Yeah, sure. We'll go see Grammy. I'll call Lilah now and see whether she can drive us over there. It's a plan."

Jeremiah nodded his thanks and sprinted for the dorms. His urgency to reread those letters was growing by the second.

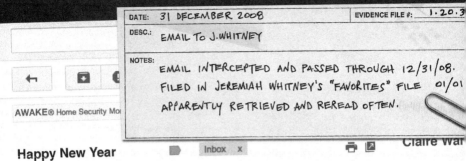

Happy New Year   Inbox x   Claire War

Claire Warren

to me

Dear Jeremiah,

Hello! I was just thinking about you and wondering how you're
doing now that Christmas has come and gone. I bet the holidays
are extra tough when you've lost someone dear to you. My heart
goes out to you.

I'm babysitting for my sister so she and her husband could go to
a work party of his in Salt Lake. It's supposed to be a big deal, so
I was happy to help out. My niece and nephew are both conked
out already. They're only five and two, so staying up until
midnight wasn't an option. ☺ I've got a sweater I'm knitting and a
couple of Jane Austen DVDs and plenty of snacks—I couldn't
think of a more peaceful way to spend the evening!

I'm sure you are wondering what I'm doing emailing you on New
Year's Eve. It's part of one of my resolutions for 2009, so why not
get a head start, right? My mom loves to quote Sister Camilla
Kimball, who apparently used to say, "Never suppress a generous thought." So that's one of my resolutions this year: to act on
thoughts, especially generous ones. ☺

I like the idea of being generous, but frankly, I'll confess that I'm a
little shy, ☺ and sometimes I'm afraid to reach out. But I thought
of you a minute ago while I was watching Persuasion, and it felt
like an impulse I shouldn't ignore. So I looked you up in the ward
directory, and here I am!

I hope that you don't mind that I've been praying for you to have
peace and comfort in your grief. I can't imagine going through
what you have endured lately. I guess that's all I wanted to say. ☺
I'll get back to Anne Eliot and Captain Wentworth now. Happy
New Year! I'll see you around, I guess.

Your Friend,

Claire Warren

CHAPTER TEN

Constance

As it turned out, they had to wait until the next night anyway. The Family History Center wasn't open on Monday nights, which made sense, Jeremiah supposed. Even senior citizens were supposed to have family home evening. Tuesday after Lilah finished her shift at the dental group where she worked as a hygienist, the three met in the cafeteria for a quick dinner, then drove downtown to the big center where Lilah's grandmother worked.

"So, Jay," Porter said, twisting around in the front passenger seat to look at him. "That girl Claire, the Rice Krispie Treat expert. The woman has skills. I think you need to break out of your slump and ask her out. Trust me: dating a woman who can cook has plenty of advantages."

Lilah took her hand off the steering wheel and gave Porter's shoulder a playful shove. She glanced at Jeremiah in the rearview mirror. "Porter's right, Jeremiah—Claire has a gift—and she's smart, too. I'm sure she likes you. What do you think? Any sparks there?"

Jeremiah didn't know how to respond. Sparks? Sure.

Claire was beautiful; what guy wouldn't feel something around her? But Jeremiah didn't think it was smart—or fair—to date anyone seriously before his mission. And Claire was definitely someone he could get serious about. But Porter was still staring at him, obviously expecting an answer.

"I don't know, you guys. I've had other things on my mind. I'll think about it, okay?"

Porter squinted at him, then nodded. "Think hard, boy. Otherwise you'll end up an old maid."

Ouch. That earned Porter another shove from Lilah, this one not quite so playful. Lilah and Porter were five years older than Jeremiah—and they still weren't married. That fact didn't seem to bother Porter at all—but it must weigh on Lilah, as an LDS woman living where they lived. Did Porter not ever think about what came out of his mouth?

Lilah parked on the street in front of a red brick chapel with fancy white trim. It must be old; modern church buildings tended to be much plainer. The winter sun had set, leaving only a stain at the horizon to mark its presence. The wind blew sharp and bitter across the valley, and Jeremiah turned up his coat collar as they got out of the car. He looked around nervously at the deserted downtown streets. Just next door to the west, a skyscraper loomed, its featureless glass walls mirroring the chilly, bleak sky.

Lilah saw Jeremiah staring up at the tall structure. "My parents call it 'the great and spacious building,'" she said. "They and a lot of other locals raised a stink when that thing was about to go up. It kind of ruins the whole historic feel of this area, doesn't it?" She nodded toward the chapel. "It's a pretty stark contrast. Some huge corporation owns it, though—GDT, I think—and all the protests couldn't do a thing against that much money."

Jeremiah shivered. A wave of cold menace seemed to roll off the structure, like mist flowing down the side of a glacier. If he stood here long enough, it would reach him— yet Jeremiah felt momentarily paralyzed, as though he couldn't escape even if he wanted to.

Then, at his back, he felt a flicker of warmth and comfort, as if someone he trusted and loved were standing right behind him. He whirled around; no one was there. Across the street stood a parking garage—another blight on the downtown ambience, he supposed. He saw no sign of life in the garage, but something good radiated out of it. Something familiar. As he took a step toward it, he noticed that Porter and Lilah were staring at him with identical puzzled expressions on their faces.

He gave them a tentative half smile. "Sorry," he said. "I just got distracted for a minute."

"It's freezing out here," Porter complained. "Let's go in where it's warm—and get you some answers."

"Absolutely." Jeremiah followed his friends inside and headed down to the basement where the Family History Center was housed.

They looked around the vast room for a minute. Jeremiah saw a sea of gray and white heads bowed over books and computer screens. How long would it take to find Lilah's grandmother?

But it turned out that she was waiting for them right near the entrance. She didn't look like a grandma, either—more like someone who would hang out at a country club than at a library full of dead people's records.

Lilah stepped forward and hugged her.

"Lilah! Hi, sweetie!"

Lilah took Jeremiah's arm and tugged him forward. "Miah, this is my grandmother, Constance Carroll. Grammy, this is Jeremiah Whitney."

Grammy looked him up and down admiringly, then stared into his eyes for several seconds. Finally she nodded, smiled, and shook Jeremiah's hand vigorously.

"Welcome!" she said with enthusiasm. "Well, you certainly are handsome. A little young for Lilah, but I feel good about you." She leaned forward conspiratorially. "Much better than that fat oaf she used to bring around." She looked at Lilah and waggled her eyebrows. "He's a keeper."

Lilah blushed. "Grammy! Jeremiah is just a friend. He's the boy I told you about the other day. I'm still dating Porter. He's right here." Lilah pulled Porter out from behind a microfiche reader. Grammy might not have seen him back there, but by the look on his face, he had heard her characterization of him, and he didn't look too happy. Jeremiah winced in sympathy.

Grammy looked over her glasses at Porter and frowned. "Oh." That was all she said, but her feelings were clear.

"Good to see you, too," said Porter, not quite keeping the sarcasm out of his voice.

Lilah jumped in before the situation could escalate.

"Grammy, we were hoping you could help Jeremiah while I show Porter the . . . Civil War census area."

Porter plastered a big, fake grin on his red face. "Yeah. I love Civil War censuses."

He thumped Jeremiah on the back, then mussed his hair. "All right, Jer-Bear, you be good for Grammy." He and Lilah walked off, probably to go find a dark corner and have a romantic moment. Had there even been a census during the Civil War years? Jeremiah shook his head. It didn't matter.

"Ah, so you're the one that's adopted?" A couple of heads turned at Grammy's slightly too-loud question, and Jeremiah took her by the elbow and pulled her over to an aisle that ran between ranks of file cabinets.

"Sshh," he said gently, and Grammy patted his arm.

"Don't be ashamed that you're adopted." She looked into his eyes again. "I can tell you're a really good kid. I can only imagine how grateful your parents must have been when they held you the first time." She paused and put a hand to her collarbone. In a quieter voice, she continued, "I feel impressed to tell you that they love you very, very much. You know that, right?"

Jeremiah couldn't speak. He recognized the truth of what she said, and an overwhelming flood of love threatened to overcome him. Grammy's next words brought him out of his reverie. "For some reason—just a crazy reason I can't explain—I took the liberty of researching your adoption." Her eyes warned him to brace himself. "It's sealed. Permanently. Legally, you'll never find out who your birth parents are. Did your adopted parents ever tell you anything about it?"

Jeremiah shook his head. "Nothing. My parents . . . passed away. I think my adoption is supposed to be a secret."

Grammy seemed to ponder that. "Yes, I feel like they kept it a secret for a reason. Any idea why?"

Jeremiah shook his head again.

"Hmmmm. Let me check with my supervisor."

Jeremiah clutched her arm again. "No, wait . . . please don't."

• • •

Constance was shocked at Jeremiah's vehemence. Young people today had such violent reactions to everything. It was clear that he wanted this to remain a secret, even if he wasn't actually ashamed of the adoption. She relaxed as she felt the Spirit stir her heart. Then she had a flash of insight. "Actually, there is something else we could try." She looked up into the boy's impossibly blue eyes. It was a shame Lilah wasn't dating him; he was gorgeous. "Have you ever heard of DNA testing?"

"No."

"Mitochondrial DNA traces your maternal line, while the Y-chromosome traces your paternal line. We might be able to find out at least where your family is from. What do you think?"

Jeremiah nodded tentatively.

"Oh, it's really neat." Constance loved the new technology and got more enthused about it every time she recommended it to someone. "You just spit in a test tube and send it out. I have a testing kit in my car. Wait here, and I'll be right back, okay?"

She turned and sped down the aisle, leaving Jeremiah alone. Lilah and her circus bear weren't anywhere near the census records, she noted absently as she left the building. She might be getting old, but she still had eagle eyes. She'd have to have a talk with that girl, and soon.

Constance locked her car after retrieving the kit and walked through the parking garage back toward the entrance of the Family History Center. Just as she left the garage, a man stepped out of the shadows and into the light of a street lamp next to the sidewalk. Constance jumped a little. This was Provo, not downtown L.A., but still. You couldn't be too careful.

"Sister Carroll."

The man had to be at least ten years older than she was. His long, white hair was pulled back into a ponytail. He had a beard, too, and while Constance generally favored the missionary look on men, she had to admit that this man didn't look like a hippie. He was clean, had a well-trimmed beard, and stood tall, his piercing blue eyes bright with intelligence. He wore work gloves, though—that was a little odd, except that it was quite cold out. He might look like someone out of *Lonesome Dove,* but she would err on the side of caution. She favored him with her most severe look.

"Do I know you? How do you know my name?"

The man pointed to her nametag. Oh, of course. The white letters were legible even in the twilight. "I need your help with something," he said. His voice was rich and full; was he a singer of some kind? That would explain the hair. "I'd be glad to help you, sir, but I'd prefer that we go inside first." Inside, where there were lots of bright lights and witnesses, and she could pull the fire alarm if need be. Constance dredged up the memory of the self-defense class she had taken at the Senior Center last summer. What were the five points of defense? Eyes, neck, instep . . . she could only remember three. That would have to be enough. She squared her shoulders.

The man put up a hand, as if to halt her train of thought. "This is about Jeremiah."

Constance narrowed her eyes. Was this why Jeremiah had been so cagey during their conversation? Did he know that people were following him? "I don't know any Jeremiah."

The stranger seemed to see right through her bluff. "The young man you've been helping."

How did he know that? Had he been stalking them inside, then followed her out here to where she was vulnerable and alone? Every nerve in her body was firing, charged with adrenaline, telling her to run. She kept up her bravado. "Okay, look. If you want to continue this conversation, you'll have to come inside." She turned away, surreptitiously putting her keys between her knuckles with the sharp edges pointing outward so she could use them as a makeshift weapon if need be.

"Stop!" His voice shocked her. She turned despite herself.

"I need you to deliver this to him," the stranger said more gently. He held out a sealed, square envelope with Jeremiah's name written on it in florid script. Constance shied away. "I'm not touching that. It could be filled with anthrax." This guy might be part of that domestic terrorist cell the authorities had just busted down in Ephraim. Constance wished for the first time that she had one of those "clapper" alarms to wear around her neck the way her friend Genevieve did.

"He needs this," the man insisted, and Constance looked into his eyes. The Spirit quieted her heart, and her fear leaked away.

The man must have seen the change in her demeanor. He softened. "How did you feel when you first met him?"

Constance thought about his question, and as she did so, a familiar peace flowed through her where there had been only fear and suspicion before. This was all right; this was supposed to happen. But she didn't give in without a fight. Her pride was at stake. "I have broken so many rules today, trying to help this young man. I have to find out what's going on."

The stranger smiled—and when he did, he looked almost familiar to her. He reminded her of someone, and the resemblance tugged at the edges of her mind. "You followed your promptings. You were supposed to help him. Jeremiah is in danger, Sister Carroll. You must give him this and tell him to be on his way." He still held the envelope out.

Constance glared at him. Why couldn't she have felt this peace earlier—why did she have to undergo heart-pounding fear first? She had to take the envelope; she knew that now. She grasped it and looked down at it. She put on her glasses so that she could inspect it more carefully.

"Okay, okay," she said. "But you know, there's this new thing called 'email.' I think you would find it much more effective than approaching old ladies in dark parking lots." She looked up to see how the handsome stranger was taking her lecture. He really ought to be ashamed of himself.

But he was gone. Constance looked around, peering into the shadows to see whether he was hiding somewhere else. But, no—he'd vanished without a trace. A gust of wind whipped through the bare trees around the chapel, and Constance hurried back inside.

• • •

Wrapped in Porter's strong arms behind the Central America stacks, Lilah peered out to check on the real reason they were here. "Where's Grammy?" She hoped Jeremiah was getting some help. Lilah hated seeing him so stressed out and afraid.

"Who cares," murmured Porter, and pulled her back into his embrace. She kissed him back happily. Oh, she loved this man, goofy bravado, sloppy habits, and all. Jeremiah and Grammy could wait.

• • •

Constance walked back to the aisle where she'd left Jeremiah. He was leaning against the filing cabinets, reading a book. Such a nice boy. The stranger had been right, though. Constance could sense danger all around him, almost like a bad, lingering smell. She touched his arm as she reached him and smiled. He looked up from his book and grinned; Constance's heart broke over his young, innocent beauty. He reminded her a little of her Harry, whom she still missed desperately, even though he had passed on years before.

"Jeremiah," she whispered around a sudden tightness in her throat. "Take this and follow the instructions." She handed him the DNA kit along with the envelope the stranger had given her. "You need to leave. Hurry."

Jeremiah looked a little surprised, and she wished she could reassure him that everything was going to be all right. But she didn't have that feeling now—just one of clear warning.

"Be careful," she said, then added, "I know you're going to find what you're looking for." She felt the Spirit confirm the truth of that, which surprised her; she hadn't even known she was going to say that.

"Oh, Grammy, there you are." Lilah's voice came from behind them. "We've been looking all over for you."

Constance turned and smiled at her granddaughter, though she could tell from Lilah's mussed hair and non-existent lipstick that she and Porter had found the archives . . . inspiring. *This isn't my first rodeo,* she wanted to tell Lilah, but kept her peace on that subject for the moment.

"Hi, sweetheart. Take him home," was all she said, motioning to Jeremiah.

Porter stepped forward and enveloped Constance in a massive bear hug. She could barely breathe, he squeezed her so tightly. Good thing she had a chiropractor's appointment scheduled for the next morning; she was going to need it.

"Take this one home, too," she directed, her voice muffled by Porter's enormous, smelly jacket. Mercifully, the oaf let her go before she suffocated.

She watched the three of them walk toward the doors. Jeremiah stopped near the exit, discovering that the envelope wasn't part of the DNA kit. What did it say? And what did the strange—but kindly—man with the long hair possibly have to communicate to this boy that he couldn't just come out and tell him himself?

• • •

Jeremiah stared at the square card. The stationery was identical to the card in his parents' van—the one that had led to all the trouble with that box. He closed his eyes against a sudden surge of rage. He wanted nothing more than to throw the card in the garbage; he wished he had done that with the first one.

He stared at the words typed on it: "Manti Road, Mile Marker 3. January 16th. 5 p.m." And handwritten at the bottom: "Come alone."

What catastrophe was in store for him this time?

SIMON ACKERMAN:

:0
SIMON: HEY, MOM. IT'S SIMON. HEY, I KNOW I WAS
JUST HOME A COUPLE OF DAYS AGO, BUT I FORGOT
SOME STUFF AND I WAS HOPING YOU COULD MAIL IT
TO ME.

:11
SIMON: I LEFT MY LUCKY SET OF PURPLE D&D DICE
IN MY SOCK DRAWER. THEY'RE IN THAT LITTLE BAG
YOU CROSS-STICHED FOR ME. AND I REALLY NEED
THEM KIND OF URGENTLY. ALSO, MY SPARE
HALBERD-WHAT? BRIAN?

:18 - 29 [SILENCE]
:29
SIMON: OH. NEVER MIND ABOUT THE HALBERD, MOM.
BRIAN SAYS IT'S ILLEGAL TO SHIP WEAPONS
THROUGH THE MAIL, SO I'LL PICK THAT UP IN
FEBRUARY. WAIT A SEC. HE'S SAYING SOMETHING
ELSE.

:34- 42 [SILENCE]
:42
SIMON. OH. HA. BRIAN WONDERED IF YOU COULD
SEND US ANOTHER BATCH OF BROOKIES. THEY'RE HIS
FAVORITE, ESPECIALLY WHEN HE NEEDS ENERGY ON
A STALK-OUT. WHAT? OUCH. QUIT IT. BRIAN.

:51
SIMON: HEY. SORRY MOM. SO YEAH. COULD YOU SEND
THOSE DICE AND MAYBE SOME NEW PARTY SOCKS AND
THE BROOKIES? THAT WOULD BE BRILLIANT. NAMA-
RIE, AMILE!

:59

***

END OF MESSAGE

CHAPTER ELEVEN

Mile Marker 3:
January 16, 2009

Jeremiah got off a Greyhound Bus on Main Street in the thriving metropolis of Helper, Utah. He had had no idea this tiny town even existed before this morning. But when he had gotten up today and made plans to get to Manti, as directed on his "invitation," he had felt like he ought to take a few extra hours and avoid the direct route. He had no idea why, but he knew better by now than to mess with his promptings. The same person who had led him to the box had made that card. He hoped today that he'd get some answers to the questions that had plagued him ever since.

He looked around. The bus driver had assured him as he dropped him off that the next bus to Ephraim would be along in a few minutes—although it was clear the guy wondered why on earth Jeremiah would want to travel to either forsaken place in the middle of the winter.

Jeremiah sat down on the sidewalk and leaned against the metal bus stop sign. He would just wait here—it was warm enough in the sun. He didn't want to risk missing the bus by stopping in at the diner across the street.

He mentally reviewed his itinerary, designed to throw off any potential pursuers. Someone had obviously followed him to Manti on his false birthday and had tracked him to Seneca Falls. He couldn't be too careful. So, today he was traveling from Helper to Ephraim, and from there to Delta.

Only when he got to Delta would he finally buy a ticket to Manti (using cash, as he would all day). If his triangulation of all the bus schedules had been accurate, that should get him to Mile Marker 3 just before 5 p.m. He had a sandwich in one coat pocket and a paperback copy of *Persuasion* in the other. It had been on his English class's reading list, and he remembered that Claire had mentioned liking it a lot. Maybe he should text her and tell her that he was reading it. No, that might seem random; maybe he'd call her tomorrow, instead. Pulling the book out, he ignored his rapidly freezing backside and started to read.

• • •

Brian peered cautiously around the door to Jeremiah and Porter's room. Coolbrith was notoriously sloppy about security; Brian took the door standing ajar as a sign that he'd schlepped off to the showers. The room was a mess, as Brian expected. Jeremiah seemed like a neat enough guy, but there was no resisting the maelstrom that was Porter Coolbrith.

Brian ducked inside; it wouldn't do for any of their neighbors to see him hovering at the door. Porter's bed was a mountainous mass of tangled blankets and pillows. He had to work quickly if Porter was in the shower. He sifted through the papers and books on Jeremiah's desk, looking for any information that might pique Megan Halling's interest. He hadn't been able to sleep very well for the past couple of weeks, lying awake tortured by thoughts of her and how he could best impress her.

She was obviously intelligent—smart enough to appreciate his keen mind. Girls like that were few and far between, Brian had found by sad experience. He had to find something to send to her so that he'd have an excuse to contact her again.

The desk was a bust. Brian turned to Jeremiah's headboard, which had a couple of shelves and drawers attached to it. That was where normal people kept important things. Not Brian himself, of course. His hiding places were much more secure than that. But Jeremiah was a straightforward, trusting soul—too trusting.

As he reached to pull one of the drawers open, he heard a muffled snort from the other bed. He froze. How had he missed that someone was in the room? Stupid, stupid, he berated himself. No spy worth his salt would have let this happen.

Panicking, he lifted Jeremiah's comforter and dived underneath, hoping Porter would roll over and go back to sleep. But no. Fate was against him. He heard the bedsprings groan under Porter's significant weight and screwed his eyes tightly shut.

"Jay. You back from the shower?"

What was it—almost 11 A.M.? How on earth did Porter stay in bed this long? What a woeful lack of self-discipline.

No wonder he was so overweight. Brian himself got up early every morning so that he could complete the Canadian Air Force's routine of calisthenics. His superior aerobic control would serve him well now. He held very still and kept his breath even and light. Then he realized that Porter, though only half awake, would probably expect an answer. He let out a low grunt, trying to match Jeremiah's natural timbre.

Porter seemed to accept that. Another naive, trusting soul with inferior instincts. But that all worked in Brian's favor.

"Can I borrow your towel? I think I left mine in P.E. class."

Brian fought back a gag. Disgusting. Coolbrith was an embarrassment. Brian grunted another answer and listened to Porter making his way out of the rat's nest of blankets on his bed.

"Hey. Lilah and I are going to mail out your DNA test today, okay? I just think it's better if no one sees you doing it."

DNA test? Bingo. Megan would have to hear about this. Brian harrumphed again and waited until Porter's heavy footfalls indicated that he'd lumbered out of the room. Without closing the door, of course. Whatever.

Brian cautiously poked his head out of the covers. Okay. Safe to move. About to throw back the comforter, he noticed an envelope taped to the underside of Jeremiah's headboard. O-ho, so Jeremiah wasn't so straightforward. This kind of secreting was elementary, but showed a little more forethought than Brian would have given him credit for. But

Jeremiah was no match for Brian's carefully honed detective skills. Brian snatched the envelope off the wood, careful to handle it only by the edges so he wouldn't leave any fingerprints, and opened it.

Manti Road, Mile Marker 3. January 16th. 5 p.m. Come alone.

Fantastic. This was exactly the kind of thing he needed to get into Megan's good graces. But January 16th—that was today. Crap. He couldn't hand deliver this; there was no time. She needed to know about this right away if it was to be of any use to her. He pulled out his phone and snapped a photo of the card, then sent the photo to Megan. There. This was better, actually. Now Brian could replace the card, and Jeremiah would never be the wiser. Happier than he'd been in days, Brian jumped up off the bed and escaped before Papa Bear could come back and discover him.

• • •

Here he was: Mile Marker 3. Jeremiah looked up the deserted country road, then down again. There wasn't a house or anything else that indicated human habitation, as far as he could see—except for the road itself, and the marker. The bus had dropped him off right on time. He scanned the unkempt fields of scrub oak that ran all the way up to the foothills. He was alone.

No, he wasn't, he realized. Almost out of nowhere, a tall, lean man who looked to be in his 70s appeared at his side. Jeremiah jumped a little; people couldn't usually sneak up on him like that.

The man had long, white hair and wore a full-length denim overcoat. He looked like an ad for rodeo equipment, or something—the rangy, independent image of the manly Old West.

Jeremiah took a step backward. The guy had appeared out of thin air without a sound, and that freaked Jeremiah out a little.

"Jeremiah," the man said.

"Who are you?" Jeremiah asked.

The man handed him another square card. This one read, "2:15:4:14—Neglect not the gift that is in thee."

What did that mean? What were the numbers for? Was this some kind of a code that he was supposed to know? He looked up and searched the man's face and got no help there. But inside, Jeremiah felt calm assurance.

The man smiled. "Follow me." He turned, clearly expecting Jeremiah to obey without hesitation. Jeremiah looked around. He didn't have many other choices, and wasn't this why he had come to Manti? He followed the man into the underbrush.

The man waited until they were abreast, then held out his right hand. "I'm Ammon. I'll explain everything, but not here. Give me your cell phone."

Jeremiah stared at him, uncertain. Why did he have to give up his phone? Was this guy somehow connected with his parents' deaths? Did he want the phone so Jeremiah would have no way to call anyone for help? Or so the authorities would have no way to trace him?

"How do I know can I trust you?"

Ammon gazed into his eyes, and Jeremiah searched his face. As he did so, he felt the Spirit's quiet voice assuring him that Ammon was trustworthy. Jeremiah relaxed, feeling the tension go out of his neck and shoulders. He pulled his phone from his pocket and handed it to Ammon.

Ammon took it, removed the battery, and hid the phone in the crack of a fallen log. Jeremiah looked around. This spot of brush looked like every other around here. How would they ever find his phone again? He consciously thrust his anxiety aside, annoyed that he had so many questions.

"Let's go," Ammon said. "The horses are waiting."

Horses? Where were they going? Wouldn't an ATV be faster? This was all so bizarre. As Jeremiah followed Ammon and got on the horse, he felt as if he were somehow traveling back in time. They rode along the foothills as the sun finished its descent behind the Canyon Mountain Range to the west. Ammon constantly scanned their surroundings. Jeremiah assumed that he was watching out for anyone who might be following them. Jeremiah decided to be more watchful himself. After all, this guy looked really old; how good could his night vision possibly be?

• • •

Lilah and Porter stood inside the post office minutes before it was due to close. Porter laboriously filled out an express mail envelope, pressing hard with his ballpoint pen to make sure that his childlike writing went all the way through the multiple copies of the form. He turned to Lilah.

"What's your address?" he whispered.

She looked at him, her mouth dropping open in surprise. Seriously? They had been dating for four years, and he didn't know her address? She'd lived in the same apartment all that time. Sometimes he was so clueless. She tried to keep the hurt out of her voice as she spoke.

"It's Jeremiah's DNA test. Just use his address," she said casually. Which was exactly the same as Porter's address. Hopefully he had *that* memorized.

Porter shushed her, looking around quickly. He leaned closer to her, and Lilah could smell Cool Ranch Doritos on his breath. He rolled his eyes and whispered, "Okay, yeah. I might as well write 'Attention, creepy British bad guys. Please tamper with my DNA test so that I'll never find out who my real parents are. Signed, your victim, Jeremiah.'"

Lilah stared at Porter, then turned away. She only knew a tiny bit about the weird stuff Jeremiah was going through, and she was glad Porter was such a loyal friend, but it ticked her off that he still didn't get it.

He sidled around her so that he was facing her again. "Using your address is to protect Jeremiah's identity."

Lilah ducked her head. Her grammy had always told her that you can't change men, so don't even waste your time trying. "Just find one whose faults you can live with," she had counseled her granddaughter many times since she had turned sixteen.

Porter had glaring faults, but almost all of them went along with his enormous strengths. Two sides of the same coin. So Porter didn't know her address. It wasn't a big deal. He knew how to make her feel special—womanly and smart and safe all at the same time. That counted for a lot.

Porter must have sensed that her resolve was weakening, because he put on the same ridiculous puppy-dog face he always did when he knew he was about to get his way. "I love you," he sing-songed, his chip breath rolling over her once more.

Lilah couldn't keep from laughing. "Awwwww," she said, taking his face in her hands. "That is so . . . lame." She grinned and kissed him, then took the envelope and pen from him and wrote her address on the form. She wondered why Grammy had thought that Jeremiah needed a DNA test anyway. She stuffed the package into the proper mail slot and walked out, Porter following her.

• • •

It was full dark now—which wasn't so late, since it was only a month after the winter solstice. Jeremiah had started the ride through the wilderness flinching at every snapped twig and unidentifiable animal noise. Danger seemed to lurk behind every rock and bush as evening's shadows deepened into night. Despite all of his precautions, Jeremiah knew that someone who was determined could have tracked him here.

But after awhile, the horse's gentle, plodding rhythm lulled him out of panic mode and into idle speculation.

Did Ammon live out here somewhere? How had he known where to find Jeremiah? What was his connection to the box and the woman Jeremiah had met at the library? Who was this guy, anyway?

Suddenly, Ammon spurred his horse into a gallop, awakening Jeremiah's fears all over again. Jeremiah's horse seemed to sense that it should follow, so it took off as well. Was someone chasing them? What was going on? Jeremiah hated the uncertainty.

He hung on for dear life as they raced through the foothills. Having visited his grandparents every summer, he had a decent amount of riding experience, but he had no illusion of control as they traveled. Ammon and the horses were in charge here. Finally they slowed down, stopping in a clearing that nestled up against a mountain. Jeremiah was somewhat familiar with the San Pitch Mountains that lay to the east of Manti. He didn't remember having seen this particular spot before, but it was hard to tell. The moon wasn't up, and there were no city lights around them.

Ammon dismounted, and Jeremiah did as well. Ammon tethered both horses to a tree and started walking.

"Where . . ." Jeremiah began, but Ammon hushed him with a single finger to his lips. He led through the thick brush, holding branches out of the way for Jeremiah.

Jeremiah followed up the steep incline. Ammon showed no signs of fatigue, but Jeremiah found himself breathing hard as he climbed. Embarrassing. The man had to be older than Grandpa Whitney.

He almost bumped into Ammon when he stopped short

in front of him. Jeremiah saw him peering into the deep shadows all around. Had he heard something? After a minute, he turned to Jeremiah.

"Jeremiah, you are to tell no one about this place," he whispered. "Only those divinely chosen are granted access. They are very few. You are one of them." He paused, a sympathetic look coming into his eyes. "Your birth father was another."

Jeremiah felt a jolt of surprise travel through him. "You knew my birth father?"

Ammon nodded. "And your adoptive father and mother." He put a gentle hand on Jeremiah's shoulder. "I am sorry about your loss."

Jeremiah turned away, frustrated as he struggled to get his emotions under control. Would it ever get any easier to talk about his parents?

Ammon squeezed his shoulder, and Jeremiah got himself together. "You are to make a record of your experience here. Thus, you must film what you are about to see."

Jeremiah took his video camera out of its case. How had Ammon known that he'd have it with him? The "invitation" hadn't said anything about bringing it along. Jeremiah wondered again how much Ammon knew about him and his habits.

He switched on the camera and held it up. Ammon turned and walked toward what looked like a solid rock wall, but as they approached it, Jeremiah could just make out a narrow fold in the stone. Ammon slid sideways through it. Jeremiah took a deep breath and followed.

Inside, the camera automatically adjusted for a slightly higher level of light. As Jeremiah stood in the doorway and panned around the room, he noticed candles burning in lanterns, creating a warm, serene glow. He felt as if he had stepped back in time or into another world entirely.

He remembered how utterly safe he felt at the temple whenever he went to do baptisms for the dead. It was almost as if the outside world, with all of its noise and chaos, simply ceased to exist when he was within those strong, white walls. This place felt the same—sacred, solemn—and also unimaginably old. He thought again of those legends about Moroni traveling through Manti, and a little shiver went down his spine.

"Come in, Jeremiah," came Ammon's voice.

The cave was small; it looked as if a natural cavity of the rock had been extended by human means. Shelves and cubbies had been dug into the solid stone walls, and piles of scrolls and other ancient-looking artifacts filled the depressions. A few stalactites hung from the ceiling, but the floor was relatively smooth. A few ancient weapons leaned against the wall in the corner. One of them, a jeweled sword, was larger than the others and looked to be in better condition. Its intricate metal surface gleamed. Simon would go nuts for this stuff.

Centered against the back wall stood three square pillars about four feet high. The box rested on the middle pillar. How had it gotten *here?*

CHAPTER TWELVE

The Box

Jeremiah's heart flooded with anger, and he lashed out at Ammon, unable to contain his questions any longer. "How do you know about me, and how do you know about my family? I mean, how do you know *anything* about me?"

Ammon reached into his pocket and drew out a torn photograph. He handed it to Jeremiah wordlessly.

Jeremiah squinted at it, and his mouth dropped open. His parents smiled for the camera, holding a small baby in their arms. In the background sat a pretty woman with olive skin and dark hair and eyes. Ammon stood next to her, looking exactly the same as he did now.

"Is this the day I was adopted?" Jeremiah whispered.

Ammon nodded once. So it was true. That adoption certificate hadn't been a fake. He hadn't gotten a single detail from his grandparents about the circumstances of his birth over Christmas. Was this why? Had they been sworn to secrecy?

He assumed the young woman was his real mother. Her high, angular cheekbones matched his own. Why had she agreed to give him up? Had she been a single mother? Jeremiah hated the fact that for every question he got answered, a hundred more sprang into its place.

"Why didn't they tell me?" he cried. "Why didn't anyone tell me?" He swallowed hard. It was easier to get angry than to give in to grief. "I could tell that something was up just by the way they looked at each other that day."

Ammon gently interrupted his diatribe. "They knew very little. However, they knew this day would come. They agreed to it the day they adopted you."

Jeremiah snorted in derision. "So they adopted me just to give me up?" He cast his eyes about the room, and the box on the central pillar caught his glance. "And that box. That damned box! What's in it?"

Jeremiah reached for it, intending to open it and expose its secrets once and for all, but Ammon stepped forward and cut him off. He loomed over Jeremiah, who realized for the first time what a large and imposing man Ammon was. He wasn't bent or diminished by age at all—in fact, his entire demeanor projected vigor and immense strength.

Somewhat subdued, Jeremiah asked, "What could be so important that it would justify the deaths of my parents?"

Ammon waited silently, staring into Jeremiah's eyes. He seemed to be waiting for something—what? Well, as far as Jeremiah was concerned, Ammon could wait on through eternity. Jeremiah was sick of this nonsense. His broken heart filled with rebellion.

"You know what? I wish that box had gotten stolen."

"It would have, had I not been there when you broke your oath and abandoned it."

Jeremiah's insides twisted. "Abandoned it." He'd dropped everything to try to help his parents get out of a demolished car before it exploded and they burned to death. He knew breaking his promise about the box had been a mistake. But no matter how many chances he was given to do things over again, he would drop that box on the snowy asphalt and run to them each and every time. This man's priorities were seriously screwed up. Jeremiah let out a short laugh.

"Well, good thing you were there to pick it up," he said, his sarcasm unrestrained. "So why me, of all people? What do I have to do with any of this? I'm nothing special."

"Jeremiah, you have no idea who you are."

The old man was right about that. "No. No, I don't. But you do!" Jeremiah's voice rose with every word. "You even know who my real father was!"

Ammon bowed his head. "I do. And it is essential that you know your father."

Jeremiah felt like punching the wall. "So why don't you tell me, Ammon? Who was he?" His angry words reverberated in the tiny cave.

Ammon waited until the echoes died away before responding. "I understand you want to know about the box, its contents and power, the calling you received, and your father." He swallowed. "To be shown these answers, you must prove yourself unconditionally trustworthy. The Lord will only entrust us with greater light when we show Him that we will not betray Him. Until then, I can tell you nothing."

Jeremiah's mouth tasted bitter. "Well, we all know that I can't be trusted. Look who has the box."

"That doesn't mean you've lost it forever." Ammon's voice was gentle; was there no end to his patience? "You will have many more opportunities to prove yourself. But unless prompted otherwise, you must not tell anyone about the box. *You must protect it.*"

Jeremiah had had enough. "I didn't ask for the box, Ammon." Was that actually this guy's real name? Who named their kid after a character in the Book of Mormon? "I don't even want it." He turned to leave the cave.

As he approached the doorway, a shadowy figure jumped in front of him. Jeremiah could see a light blinking on the man's earpiece. Before Jeremiah could do anything, the man raised a gun and fired. The shot was deafening. Jeremiah swiveled just in time to see Ammon fall to the cave floor. He ran to him and knelt.

"Ammon, Ammon!" He shook the old man's shoulder. No response.

The assassin grabbed Jeremiah's shoulder and pulled him up to his feet. "Pick up the box," he ordered, motioning to the pillar.

"No!" He struggled against the man's grasp, wary of the gun that was all too close to him. He tried to twist away, but the man was too strong. As Jeremiah fought, the camera fell to the ground.

"Pick up the box!" the assassin screamed, trying to force

Jeremiah's hands toward the object. Jeremiah jerked away, and the man's bare hands touched the box instead. Blinding light flared, and the man let out a howl. All Jeremiah could see were green flashes burned into his retinas. As his vision gradually returned, he realized that the assassin sprawled unconscious on the floor. The man's chest still rose and fell, though. He looked from Ammon to his assassin and back again. What was he supposed to do now?

He heard a voice as familiar to him as his own. It was his mother whispering something in the darkness. A twinge of hope lightened his heart for a moment. After all his bad behavior, he was still worthy to hear her voice? He quieted his breath to hear her better.

"Listen."

Jeremiah stilled in a moment. He knew he had to obey.

"Jeremiah, listen." The voice was no longer that of his mother, but he knew it just as well. It was . . . saying something unthinkable.

"Jeremiah, you must slay him. You must take his life."

What?

No way. This could not be real. Jeremiah may have been named after an Old Testament prophet, but times had changed; the Lord didn't ask people to do stuff like that anymore. Did He?

The whisper continued, gentle but firm, piercing him to his core. "My ways are not your ways. You must slay him."

How could he commit cold-blooded murder? The man was just lying there—yes, he had shot Ammon and probably deserved to die, but now he couldn't even defend himself in a fair fight. Shouldn't he be arrested and brought to trial instead? Wasn't that what the Constitution was for? Jeremiah had to find a way out of this.

But the voice came a third time, unrelenting and calm. "You must do this thing. Jeremiah, my son. Have faith."

Jeremiah stood, a sensation of light and strength flowing through his veins, despite his fear and horror. The voice was clear, and the peace that he felt starting to chip away at his massive anxiety was the same peace he had come to know so well over the years. This was the Lord speaking to him. He had no doubt of that. He just doubted that he could follow this time.

He thought of Nephi, commanded to kill the drunken Laban. Had this been how it was for him? He glanced toward the corner of the cavern. That big, jeweled sword still stood there. He walked over and contemplated it. Despite its ancient appearance, the metal was bright and looked freshly sharpened. It would do the job. He picked it up, astonished at the heft of it. He returned to the fallen assassin, trying to quell the nauseating fear that threatened to well up again.

The voice still rang in his ears, and he doubted he would ever forget the way it had laid his soul open with a few simple words. *Slay him. Kill a man.* It was insane. Things like this didn't happen in the world today. But Jeremiah knew it was right.

He fell back against one of the pillars, weak with the enormity of what was being asked of him. He had never even gotten into a fight at school, had never even punched anyone. This act of violence required someone of action, someone like Porter. It was so far beyond him, he couldn't imagine it.

Yet he must do it.

The assassin stirred. Soon he would awaken. Jeremiah had to act now. Sobbing, shaking his head, he hefted the sword with both hands. He raised it as high above his head as he could and, letting out a desperate yell, he plunged it into the man's ribcage.

The man's legs jerked in a sickening fashion, then lay still. Jeremiah fell back, dropping the sword with a clatter. He watched dark blood slowly leak out from under the man. Jeremiah sat with his back against a pillar, chest heaving, fighting the strong urge to empty his stomach onto the cave floor.

• • •

A cough came from behind him, startling him badly. He turned. Ammon was alive! He crawled to the old man's side, all of his earlier anger and frustration dissipating in a moment. He nearly wept with relief as Ammon opened his eyes. He raised himself up on his elbows and looked past Jeremiah to the corpse beyond. Jeremiah knelt next to him, still shaking as he looked at Ammon's chest. It was a miracle. He knew the assassin's bullet had hit Ammon; why wasn't he bleeding?

Ammon squeezed Jeremiah's arm. "Jeremiah, I am sorry."

One last seed of rebellion rose up within Jeremiah, and

he had to let it out before it started to fester. "I thought you said the Lord only permitted those chosen to enter into this place."

Ammon sat up all the way. "That's correct. Search him."

Jeremiah's stomach lurched at the thought, but he obeyed after a moment. Searching carefully through the man's pockets, he found only a cell phone—no identification, no money, nothing. Was the cell phone what he was supposed to find? He opened it and looked at its glowing blue screen.

"Msg: B. Lanton," it read. "Submit status report on op. Limit: 48 hours." This was followed by a short string of numbers and letters.

"Op?" Was murdering Ammon and Jeremiah and stealing the box this guy's "op?" Jeremiah pressed the Start button to look for more information, but the phone was password protected.

Ammon leaned over so that he could see the screen as well. "In time we will know why. Just remember: whatever the Lord requires is right, no matter the cost."

Jeremiah stared at the phone's screen, his vision blurry with tears. He felt his mother's presence all around him, as warm and soft as one of her famous hugs.

"Everything will be all right," she whispered. Jeremiah closed his eyes, savoring the feeling of her nearness. He yearned to believe those words. Yes, everything would be all right. Despite the awful thing he'd just done, he felt the truth of that sink into his bones.

remember Robert Robinson

1.9.7.12

CHAPTER THIRTEEN

Call on Him Often

Jeremiah slung Ammon's right arm around his shoulders and helped him limp out of the cave. The tall man was heavy, but fortunately seemed to be gaining strength with every step. It was dark, so Jeremiah couldn't tell for sure, but Ammon didn't seem to be bleeding, either. How and why had he been prepared to take a gunshot to a chest? Did he have on some sort of bulletproof vest under his denim coat?

"Stop here," the old man directed. They leaned against a boulder while Ammon regained his breath. The moon had risen, but the pale shadows it cast made the night feel as dark as ever. Every little sound in the brush made Jeremiah jump with fright. Had the assassin been alone, or did he have partners hiding out here somewhere? Overwhelmed, he let his head sink down to his chest.

"I'm sorry," he said to Ammon. "This is all my fault."

Ammon opened his coat and took a small copy of the Book of Mormon out of his breast pocket. He held it out in the moonlight to Jeremiah, who could see that a bullet had gone more than halfway through it. Ammon opened the book, rifling its pages until the spent bullet fell out into the long grass at their feet.

"There is protection in the scriptures," Ammon said. Jeremiah looked up and realized he was making a joke. He gave a tentative half smile.

Ammon went on more seriously, addressing Jeremiah's fearful confession. "There are only two that I know of who walked on water. Christ was one, Peter the other.

"But Peter failed. His fear of the wind overcame his faith. But when Peter failed, he still had the sense to call on the Lord. And the Lord reached forth his hand and caught Peter immediately." He paused for a second.

Jeremiah thought about that story. It was true; Peter had enthusiastically accepted Jesus' challenge, only to falter and nearly drown. But Jesus had saved him and had loved and later trusted him, regardless of his momentary panic and lack of faith.

God was no respecter of persons; Jeremiah had to believe that the Lord felt the same way about him as He had about Peter.

"Jeremiah, you had the box, but you lost it. How often do you call on the Lord through your prayers?"

Jeremiah felt his cheeks get hot and was grateful for the cover of darkness for once. Ever since his parents' deaths, his prayers had been slipshod or nonexistent. He knew in some obscure way that he was angry at God for taking them from him, and perhaps subconsciously he had decided to punish God in return by refusing to speak to Him. Parsing it out in his mind like that made him realize how foolish and shortsighted his reasoning had been.

"You have to qualify yourself to be worthy of the box," Ammon said. "When you demonstrate your faith to the Lord, He'll immediately reach out to protect you."

Jeremiah set his jaw. What—killing a man wasn't enough proof of Jeremiah's loyalty and obedience? And this whole thing with the box—could it possibly be anywhere near as important as the mission Jesus had had for His apostle?

"He has no obligation to me. I broke His trust."

"Sometimes the Lord very literally reaches out to save us." He held up the Book of Mormon, then offered it to Jeremiah, who reluctantly took it from him and put it in his own coat pocket.

"Many times, He works through others. If you take the time to look, you'll be surprised by how many in your life have been placed there to help you." Ammon paused, looking at Jeremiah closely. "You are only alone if you choose to be."

That last statement, though uttered gently, cut Jeremiah to the quick. Ammon had no idea how hard these last weeks had been for him. He swallowed his pride and nodded. Ammon clapped him on the shoulder and winced. Even though the bullet hadn't penetrated his skin, the force of it must have bruised, if not broken, some ribs. Jeremiah wondered whether they should go to the emergency room. Ammon turned and briskly descended the slope toward the spot where they had left the horses.

As Jeremiah followed, he wondered about the body of

the man he'd killed. Was he one of the people who had set fire to Jeremiah's house? Would Ammon come back and bury him? How would he clean the blood up off the porous stone floor? Would the authorities notice the man missing from society? What about his employers—he couldn't believe that the man had acted alone, even if he had come to the cave without any help. Would they be able to trace his killing back to Jeremiah somehow?

Questions chased themselves around his mind as he and Ammon rode back to where his cell phone was hidden, then on to the mile marker. Just as they arrived by the side of the road where they had first met, a Greyhound bus pulled up and stopped. With a hiss, its doors opened, and the driver looked inquiringly at Jeremiah.

Jeremiah looked at Ammon, who motioned him forward. "This bus will get you home—by a more direct route than the one you took here," he said with a wink. "Go home and rest. And pray," he said, raising a finger. He looked at the bus driver and nodded.

"But I have so many questions," Jeremiah protested.

"I have often felt that questions are more important than answers." Ammon raised a hand as if to forestall any further argument. "But in time, as you are faithful, you will know more. I promise."

Jeremiah nodded, overwhelmed with fatigue and resignation. With one last look at Ammon, he dismounted the horse and got on the bus. "I don't have a ticket," he told the driver. The man handed him a small triplicate form he pulled from a shelf on the dashboard. "Fill this out and mail in your payment," he said. "Have a seat. I have a schedule to keep."

When Jeremiah finally got back to his dorm, he felt like he'd been gone for a century. His room was dark; Porter must be out with Lilah. He tossed his coat on his bed. As he did so, Ammon's copy of the Book of Mormon fell out of the pocket and onto the floor with a soft thump. Jeremiah picked up the book and flipped through its pages, glancing at random verses as he did so. He remembered Ammon's final words and got to his knees. He lay his face on his forearms, but flinched as he put weight on his cheek. The assassin had cuffed him a good one; Jeremiah wondered whether he had a black eye. He raised his head slightly, then bowed it humbly.

"Father, forgive me," he whispered. "I have been rebellious, proud, and angry. And I did something horrible tonight—even though I'm sure that Thou didst tell me to do it—right? If Thou couldst confirm that, it would be great." He waited, listening carefully, dismissing random thoughts one by one from his mind so he could hear clearly. After a moment, gentle warmth stole over him, and his heart felt lighter. Yes. It had been awful, but it had been right.

"Father, I thank Thee that I am alive. I thank Thee that Ammon is alive, and I thank Thee for giving me another chance." He paused. "Please tell me what to do next."

His forearms were resting on his coat, and deep inside one of his pockets, something vibrated repeatedly. Startled, he reached into the pockets and pulled out the phone. It wasn't his; it was the assassin's. The screen flashed a request for a password.

He could feel that he needed the password. But how could he know what it was? "Help me," he said silently, and as he did so, Ammon's words came into his mind. "There is protection in the scriptures."

He picked up the Book of Mormon again and opened it. Moving quickly, he found his way to the first page the bullet hadn't penetrated. It was Helaman chapter one, verse twelve. A brown sear marked the name "Kishkumen." Jeremiah's heart thudded. It had the right number of letters for the password. Marveling, he typed in the word and hit "Enter."

Success. The screen immediately changed, and Jeremiah gazed down at a guy in a room. With a shock, he realized that he was seeing himself from behind. A hidden camera? Someone had been spying on him? Suddenly he felt like an animal in a cage at the zoo. How long had people been watching him?

It made sense that the assassin had known exactly where to find him. He twisted around and looked up—on the smoke alarm in the corner of the ceiling over Porter's bed, he saw a tiny black button. He never would have noticed it otherwise.

He stood and jumped onto Porter's bed. His fingers just reached the smoke alarm. He stepped on a stuffed elephant Lilah had given Porter, trying to get a fraction of an inch more height. There—got it. He ripped it off the smoke alarm and tossed it to the floor. He jumped down and ground it to tiny shards of plastic beneath his heel. He checked the phone; the screen showed static. *Good.*

But who else was receiving the feed to that camera? Who had just learned that Jeremiah knew he was being hunted?

Re: Maternity Leave

To see messages related to this one, group messages by conversation.

From: brenna.lanton@zoobynews.com

To: z@gdt.com

Dear Z,

Thanks for your reassurances regarding the time I'm taking off next month to have this baby. My husband and I appreciate the company's generosity regarding the paid leave; we recognize that a benefit of that magnitude is almost unheard of in this global economy, and we are very grateful.

I just wanted to state in writing that I have absolute confidence in my ability to monitor Ms. Halling and the Whitney situation even while I am at home and recovering. Certainly, with the marvelous technology available, especially given the magnitude of the company's resources, working remotely in an effective manner should not be a problem at all.

Please consider my request to retain oversight on this case during my leave. I believe my record speaks for itself: there is no one more qualified or more motivated to bring this project to fruition.

Please let me know your thoughts on this matter at your earliest convenience.

Brenna
Faculty Coordinator
Zooby News

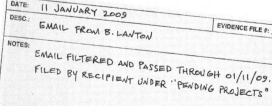

DATE: 11 JANUARY 2009
DESC.: EMAIL FROM B. LANTON
EVIDENCE FILE #: 2.3.21.3
NOTES: EMAIL FILTERED AND PASSED THROUGH 01/11/09. FILED BY RECIPIENT UNDER "PENDING PROJECTS"

CHAPTER FOURTEEN

Promises

Jeremiah walked into the common room, his arms full of party decorations. The RAs recycled them for every occasion; it seemed like every week, someone or other was getting his mission call. Brian stood in the corner with Simon, blowing up balloons. In the center of the room, a girl stood on a stepladder, trying to keep her balance as she hung strips of twisted crepe paper. With a pleasant twinge in the pit of his stomach, he realized it was Claire.

She looked down and smiled at him as he crossed the room to her. "Hey!" she said.

"Oh, hi," he answered as casually as he could. As he looked at her, he felt a stillness in his core, and immediately Ammon's words from the day before echoed in his ears. "There will be many placed in your path to help you." He looked at Claire with new eyes. He already realized that God put Porter in his life for a reason. Could the same be true with Claire? He was staring at her, and she was blushing a vivid shade of deep rose. He looked down at the streamers in his arms.

"Oh, um," Claire said. "Could you do me a favor?"

Jeremiah set his burden down on a table and climbed up the stepladder until he was just beneath her. She was too short for this job; even though he stood a step lower, he took the streamer from her hand and easily taped the crepe paper to the ceiling. Claire looked over her shoulder at him, her eyes bright. "That's actually not what I had in mind, but . . . thanks," she said, laughing a little. Jeremiah grinned back at her, but then Claire's eyes widened in surprise.

"What happened?" she asked, and Jeremiah realized that she was looking at the bruise on his cheek. He involuntarily touched his face. He hadn't come up with a cover story for it.

"Oh." He scrambled for an explanation. He couldn't exactly say that he'd been injured in a brawl with someone he'd then killed. "Um, horse accident," he finished lamely. "Not a big deal. It's fine." He was anxious to change the subject. "So, what did you need?"

Just then, Porter and Lilah came in, carrying a large, butcher-paper banner with "Congrats, Elder Everett" painted on it. Lilah must have made it; the letters looked professionally done. There seemed to be no end to Lilah's diverse talents, and Jeremiah thought for the hundredth time how lucky Porter was to have her.

Porter looked up at Jeremiah and Claire, who mercifully had her back to him. Porter made a smoochy face at Jeremiah, and he glared back. *Don't embarrass me.* He sent an urgent brainwave to his roommate, who grinned as if he'd received it loud and clear—but planned to ignore it.

Claire seemed unaware of the exchange. She only had

eyes for Jeremiah, which was more than a little intoxicating. At this close range, he could smell her shampoo and something else . . . maybe it was vanilla. Was it a perfume, or was it the lingering aroma of something she'd baked? She broke his reverie. "I was wondering whether you could teach the FHE lesson on Monday." *Oh.* Was that it? Jeremiah had hoped that Claire might need something that would require spending time together. Still, maybe he could do the favor and use it as a bridge toward asking her out on a date. His earlier resolutions not to start a relationship were starting to feel immature and shortsighted. Jeremiah realized that he didn't want Claire to lose interest in him.

He cast his mind over his schedule. As he did so, he saw Megan Halling walk in with some sparkling cider. Fancy— the dorm didn't have the budget for treats like that. *Who's she trying to impress?* He kept thinking about what Claire had asked; Monday was sticking in his brain, for some reason. Old Testament class, Business Math . . . oh, right. *Crap.*

Normally, he couldn't think of anything that would compete with saying yes to Claire's request, but his favorite band was playing within walking distance on Monday night. That didn't happen every day, and he had been planning on splurging on a ticket and going. Now he had a full-on dilemma on his hands.

"Next Monday?" he asked aloud. "Elizabethan Report is having this secret album release show." Megan was lingering nearby; was she eavesdropping on their conversation? Why would she do that? Jeremiah ignored her and turned his attention back to Claire, regretting immediately that he'd said anything about the band.

She nodded and smiled, but Jeremiah could tell she was disappointed. He hated that he'd been the cause of that sad look on her face. *Helping her is more important than the concert,* the Spirit whispered. He realized that he agreed.

"But actually, you know what? Tickets are really hard to get." Not to mention that he couldn't afford to go. "And I should probably be more involved with stuff like that. So, yeah." Megan had moved back toward the exit and was fiddling with her cell phone's earpiece. Maybe she wasn't staying for the party.

"Really?" Claire said. "Okay, thank you!"

Jeremiah hadn't taught Family Home Evening before—at least, not with anyone other than his parents. He looked around the room nervously. There could be as many as forty people there. He had no idea how to keep them entertained and, hopefully, give them a spiritual uplift at the same time. He glanced at Claire. She'd taught the lesson at least twice last semester—probably because, as Family Home Evening Coordinator, she hadn't been able to get anyone else to do it.

Inspiration hit him. "Um, actually," he said. "Would you be interested in, I don't know, teaching together?"

Claire's face lit up again. He loved it when that happened. "Yeah!"

"Really?" Jeremiah realized that he was grinning like a chimpanzee in front of just about everybody he knew, but he didn't care.

"Yeah, that would be great!"

Porter stepped over. "Hey, lover-boy."

Lilah elbowed him sharply. "Porter!" she admonished, but he remained unfazed. He was shameless.

"D'you guys have any extra Scotch tape?" he asked. Claire eased her way down the stepladder past Jeremiah. "I'll go grab some."

Lilah stepped forward. "I'll help her." She followed Claire, but looked over her shoulder at Porter as she left the room. She wiggled her fingers at him; Jeremiah had no idea what that might mean, but Porter seemed to understand, giving her a thumbs-up in return. He looked up at Jeremiah.

"So, Lilah thinks you need to ask out Claire. Like, now. She wants you . . ."

Jeremiah got down to floor level and looked at his roommate. Porter's eyes darkened as he saw Jeremiah straight on. "Dude, your face looks like crap. Who beat you up?"

Jeremiah looked around nervously. A few feet away, Brian was staring at them. He must have heard Porter's question. He leaned close to Porter and whispered, "Some guy followed me to Manti."

Porter looked at him long and hard. "How'd he know you were going?"

"I got his phone." Jeremiah pulled the phone out of his pocket, turned it on, and held it out so that Porter could see the photo of the Manti "invitation." Jeremiah's theory was that the assassin had photographed it and returned it to its hiding place at the same time that he had placed the hidden camera in their dorm room.

"What happened to him?" Porter asked.

Jeremiah couldn't meet his roommate's eyes. Porter obviously misunderstood his shame for fear.

"If someone's trying to hurt you, I'm gonna kill him."

Jeremiah glanced at Porter's grin. For a single, stomach-flopping second, he thought that Porter had guessed what he'd done. But then he realized that his friend was just trying to cheer him up.

. . .

On the other side of the room, Megan got on the phone with Brenna. If she could score two passes to that concert, Jeremiah would be putty in her hands. Her employers were unimaginably well connected; they could pull the necessary strings if she could convince them of the need.

"You get the passes; I'll get him there," she murmured. *Awesome.* She could see a fabulous promotion—and help for her father—in her very near future. She was going to bag the story on Jeremiah and that box if it took everything she had.

She strode across the room and nudged Jeremiah playfully. He looked like he and Coolbrith were having an intense moment; it was time to lighten the situation. Coolbrith glared at her, then said pointedly, "I'm gonna go help Lilah." He gave Jeremiah a meaningful glance then stomped away.

Fat hypocrite. Megan couldn't stand RMs like him, always watching and judging, always with secret desire behind their cold eyes. She preferred her men more intriguing. *Like Jeremiah.* He was a bit wet behind the ears, but Megan felt herself drawn to the mystery behind his gorgeous, somehow exotic face. She wondered about his ethnicity—did he have some Latin blood? That would explain the dark hair and those delicious cheekbones—which were devastating when paired with his piercing blue eyes.

And where had he gotten the awful bruise on his cheek? It only added to his mystery and charm. What's more, he knew more than he was saying about his parents' murder; Megan could feel it in her journalistic bones.

"So," she said, switching into full coquetry mode. She leaned forward conspiratorially. "I've got two backstage press passes for the Elizabethan Report concert on Monday. Know anybody who'd want to go with me?"

The poor boy lit up like a Christmas tree. Oh, this was way too easy.

"Yeah, I love that band . . ." he said, a little too loudly. Then his face fell. "But, I promised." He looked at her, apology in his eyes. "I'm supposed to teach FHE on Monday."

When she realized he was serious—not just playing hard to get—Megan just barely restrained herself from bursting into incredulous laughter. No wonder Claire had the hots for him; this kid was a total Peter Priesthood. Far too good to be true. What tactic to take? Lighthearted persuasion seemed to be in order.

"FHE comes every week," she said casually, then pressed herself against his arm. *Mmm, nice muscles,* she noted absently. "You'll hate yourself if you miss this concert." She let him ponder that nugget for a few seconds.

"You're probably right," he said, looking like he was

going to give in. Then he flip-flopped again. "But the thing is, I promised."

"Really?" Megan said, pouting a little. It was time to tap into his instinct to rescue. He was clearly a good little do-bee; playing damsel in distress should work. Going with her would be "the right thing to do." She just had to convince him of that.

Then that numbskull paranoiac Brian walked over and ruined everything. Beyond him, she could see his half-wit, redheaded roommate—what was his name? Steven? No—Simon, that was it. She gave Brian her most imperious "be-gone" squint, but he wasn't buying it today.

"Megan, we need to talk. Now."

"Right now?" Megan stalled. Jeremiah was on the brink of agreeing to go to the concert, she could sense it. If she walked away now, Claire might get her little white milk teeth sunk back into him. But Brian did not look like he was going to leave her alone until she gave him what he wanted. *Fine.*

"Well, I won't take 'no' for an answer," she said, smiling up at Jeremiah. "So I'll be right back."

Brian clamped his soft, white hand on her wrist and pulled her into the hallway. They made for the first door on the right—the men's room, Megan noticed with growing amusement.

Once they were inside, Brian stopped at the bank of sinks and stared at her. Finally, he whispered through gritted teeth, "What did you do with that picture I sent you?"

What? Why the cold feet? What had happened to spook Spooky?

"Bold move, Brian," she said with a laugh, glancing around the room. "I don't know what you're talking about." As her voice reverberated against the tiles, a toilet flushed. Disgusting. She couldn't believe Brian had brought her in here—but then it got worse. As the occupant of that stall exited, Brian dragged her into an adjoining stall and shut the door.

"What are you doing?" Megan squealed. This was absurd.

Brian shushed her furiously, then hissed, "Someone got that picture I gave you about Manti. And they hurt Jeremiah. You saw his face."

Brian stared intently at her. *Crap.* She hadn't connected Jeremiah's bruises with her passing that photo on to Brenna. She had to be careful with this crafty little conspiracy geek—he was too smart for his own good. This was DEFCON 5; it was time to pull out all the stops.

She burst into loud tears and threw herself onto his shoulder, wrapping her arms around him and holding on for dear life. In shock, he nearly fell over backward, then regained his balance and hesitantly put his arms around her in return. She could feel his hands stealing around her waist. *Perfect.*

"I'm so embarrassed," she sobbed. "It's just that . . . my purse was stolen, and that picture was in it. I just wanted to use it to help Jeremiah."

Behind her, the stall door creaked as someone tried to

open it. He let go of her and bent down to see who was out there. She crouched, too. Suddenly Simon's face dropped into view from above. His guileless blue eyes went wide with concern. Brian stood up just as Simon swung the door open. The Red Elf glared at his roommate with outrage.

"You filthy cur!" Simon cried. He turned to Megan with courtly concern. "Did he try to kiss you on the lips?" he asked in an undertone.

"No!" Brian shouted. Simon quelled him with a severe look. Oh, he was priceless, this one.

"A true gentleman never makes a lady cry. That's the Seventh Rule of Chivalry."

Megan heard the main bathroom door creak open yet again. This was turning into a circus. Who knew that the freshman dorm men's room was the true Crossroads of the West? Brian yanked Simon into the stall and shut the door again.

Megan dabbed at her crocodile tears; she hoped to avoid runny mascara if at all possible.

With a flourish, Simon presented her with a pressed linen handkerchief. *You've got to be kidding,* she thought. *What century is this kid from?* But she smiled and batted her lashes as she accepted it, knowing that she was wrapping him around her pinkie finger as she did so. Another plan began to form in her mind.

"If we don't protect Jeremiah, no one will. We have got to find a way to keep track of him all the time, so that if he ever gets in trouble again, we can help him."

She fastened her gaze upon Simon imploringly, then turned it on Brian. They were both helpless.

"Brian's button is a spy camera!" Simon volunteered enthusiastically.

"Simon!" Brian muttered, but Elf Boy went on.

"We could hide it on Jeremiah, and that way we could always see where he is!" Triumph lit up his face. He might be clueless most of the time, but he was right; that was a great idea. Megan scooched herself even closer to Brian and put her hand on his shoulder. She fixed him with her best pouty, hopeful look, and he was a goner. He nodded, as if hypnotized.

"Okay. Give me your phone, and I'll sync the camera to it."

He deserved a reward; this was better than Megan had hoped for. Where did he get all his crazy spy gear, jamesbond.com? Come to think of it, Megan should get the URL from him at some point.

"You're perfect—perfect," she pronounced. Brian simpered at the compliment. Out of the corner of her eye, she could see Simon hovering between outraged jealousy and resigned defeat. *Good.* She could use that later.

• • •

Jeremiah looked around the room. The party had started; Hunter stood in the middle of the room, surrounded by a pack of eager friends, his unopened mission call envelope in his hands. Megan walked in, followed at a short distance by Brian and Simon. Huh. That was odd; Brian and Simon looked like they had been arguing, which was unusual for them. Megan sauntered right up to Jeremiah. She was sexy; there was no denying it. Just looking at her made him flush.

"Jeremiah," she murmured. "Elizabethan Report! They probably won't be in Provo again for years. FHE? Will always be here." She winked at him, then pouted prettily. "Join me? I don't want to go alone."

Jeremiah looked down at her. He could smell her perfume—something exotic and expensive-smelling—different from Claire's wholesome aroma, but just as interesting. He looked across the room at Claire, who must have sensed him, because she looked up and smiled at him at just that second.

Megan followed his gaze and squeezed his arm. "She's not going anywhere either."

Jeremiah thought about it. He might never have a chance to see this band again—let alone get backstage. It was the kind of opportunity fans lived for. There was no way he could pass it up. He could always teach another Monday; after all, as Megan had said, FHE came every week. He looked at Megan and grinned.

Nodding, he said, "Okay. Yeah."

Megan leaned up on her toes and kissed him softly on the cheek.

• • •

Upstairs in Jeremiah's room, Brian picked up Jeremiah's navy duffel coat. He wore it all the time, though Brian had

heard him comment about how much warmer the winter in
Utah seemed than the winters back east. The dark coat would
act as perfect camouflage for the spy-cam button. Brian se-
cured it at the edge of the collar, then checked the image
on Megan's phone. Excellent. It was working perfectly—
definitely worth the money he'd spent on it. Carefully, Brian
arranged the coat on the back of Jeremiah's desk chair just
the way it had been, then stole back downstairs to rejoin the
party and give Megan his report.

CoolRock IM with Smilah

Hiya, gorgeous.

 Hey, P!

Fun party tonite. Thx 4 ur help on the signage.

No prob, hun. It was fun.

Ur the best girlfriend ever.

Glad you think so! Everything okay?

I guess. Worried about J.

Yeah, he's had a tough time of it.

Gotta get him out of his dang shell. Seems like he's getting worse, not better.

I could make him some treats.

Methinks he need a diff sort of treat = girl = CLAIRE. Don't think he got my hints tonite.

☺ They were pretty strong hints.

Yeah, right? Any fool can tell she = jonesing for him.

☺She's sweet. They'd make an adorable couple.

Yeah. I think I = taking matters into my own hands. Gotta plot this out. C-ya, babe.

Sweet dreams, P. I <3 U.

Me 2 xoxoxoxo

CHAPTER FIFTEEN

Secret Combinations

Porter walked into the dorm room, intentionally making his footsteps heavier than usual. He carried a cafeteria tray before him. He looked at Jeremiah, who lay curled up in his blankets like a bedbug. He'd seemed fine the day after he got back from Manti, but after that, he had retreated into his shell, acting even weirder than he had right after his parents were killed.

Lilah thought maybe it was delayed grief that was causing Jeremiah to shut down; it had to take more than a few weeks to get over trauma like that. But Porter felt like there was something else going on, and if he didn't intervene, Jeremiah might end up blowing off the entire semester.

Porter had learned the hard way that cutting classes was a very slippery slope. He wasn't going to stand by and let his best friend make the same mistakes he had made. Enough was enough. It was time to take the gloves off. He set the cafeteria tray on Jeremiah's headboard with a clatter.

"C'mon, Jay. It's 1:30. Breakfast time. Time to quit skipping out on life."

No response. Porter removed an orange, a mini cereal box, and a milk carton from his coat pocket and slammed each item onto the tray. Then he crossed to his bed and flopped down on his mattress.

"Come on, dude! You're going on day four of this! Do you know how hard it was for me to sneak this stuff out of the Commons for you?"

Again with the stone wall. Porter decided it was time to fight dirty.

"Maybe I should have brought you baby food instead." No reaction. *Dang.* The baby-taunting always worked on his slacker junior companions on his mission. Finally, he shouted in exasperation, "What's going on, bro?"

Movement. *Aha.* Jeremiah sat up, turned around, and looked at Porter. His eyes were red-rimmed, and his cheeks were sunken. *Crap, he looks like death.* Maybe Porter should drag Jay's sorry bum down to the medical center and have him tested for strep, or something.

"Do you remember that guy I told you about?" Jeremiah asked. Porter thought for a moment. Jay must be talking about that trip to Manti again. *Oh, yeah. The phone.* He nodded, waiting for more.

"I killed him."

It took every ounce of manly control for Porter to keep his jaw from dropping to the floor. What on earth? "Are you serious?"

Jeremiah sat silently, looking like he'd been hounded by a mob of ghosts. No wonder. This was major.

"I didn't want to do it. But I had to."

Okay, whoa. They were getting into crazyland, here. He *had* to kill someone? A bolt of uneasiness blossomed in Porter's chest. "What do you mean, you had to?" He waited, more and more certain that Jeremiah was going to pull a knife out from under his comforter and lunge at him. They'd both end up the main story on stupid Megan Halling's Zooby News show, and the terrorists would win.

Then—he felt a warmth surround him like a hug from a dear friend, and he heard the echo of Jeremiah's mother's whispers sound in his mind again. "Protect him." *Okay. Fine.* He'd try to keep an open mind.

"God commanded me to," Jeremiah confessed.

And incredibly, Porter knew he was right. His brain still balked, but his heart told him his friend was okay. "That's really Old Testament-type stuff." He paused, looking within himself. Everything he'd ever learned about the Spirit— mostly on his mission or in the temple—confirmed that Jeremiah was no murderer. "You're sure you had to do it, though, right?"

Jeremiah's chin sank to his chest. "Yeah, I'm sure."

Porter understood now—the days of self-imposed misery Jeremiah had been undergoing—and unintentionally inflicting on his most patient and long-suffering roommate. Jeremiah was putting himself through hell for something he didn't need to suffer for.

"If you're sure, then what are you worried about?" Porter knew he wasn't much of a "shades of grey" thinker.

To him, the world had always been pretty much black and white—and that was the way he liked it.

"Just because God commanded it doesn't make it any easier," Jeremiah said, anger flaring in his eyes. Porter had seen that look before, in the eyes of junior comps. It was a look that displayed defiance, but secretly begged for direction. Porter knew how to handle this. They would muscle their way through—together.

"Come on, man. You're coming up to campus with me." He stood, expecting exact obedience. Jeremiah did not comply.

"No."

Porter sat back down on his bed. Jeremiah didn't look like he was going anywhere with Porter. And actually, that was probably okay Porter decided, after catching a whiff of Jay at close proximity. Usually Jeremiah was Mr. Personal Hygiene, but right now, Porter's nose told him that his buddy was in serious need of a shower.

"I'm not going up to campus," Jeremiah said, sounding like a five-year-old with a bee in his . . . bonnet. "All those kids," he said, his voice gradually filling with frustration and rage. "All they think about is their midterms, or who they're going to ask out this weekend. All I do is think about what I did." Overcome, Jeremiah let himself fall back down on his mattress.

Fine. Porter could see how this was going. Jay needed a little more time to wallow in guilt. Understandable. Porter would let him have his way—for now. A plan quickly formed in his mind. He pulled a theater ticket out of his pocket and set it on the cafeteria tray. Lilah would understand; he'd take her to the play a different night—or to a different show altogether.

"I have to go to this play tonight for class, and you're coming with me. I got you a ticket." No response; it seemed as though Jeremiah had returned to the playground of catatonia.

"I'm serious," he insisted to the back of Jeremiah's head. "*Rockwell* serious. Okay? You'd better be there at 7:15. I won't be stood up." He looked up and down the length of Jeremiah's prostrate form, sighed, and left. He wondered whether Lilah had any brownies at her apartment, because he was in serious need of some sustenance.

• • •

Jeremiah entered the theater a few minutes before the play was supposed to start. He scanned the throng for the unmistakable hulk that was Coolbrith, but Porter was nowhere in sight. Instead, he saw someone in the middle of the foyer waving in his direction—Claire.

A thrill ran down Jeremiah's spine at the sight of her. She was so pretty. She radiated purity and hope and everything good. He descended the staircase, and she met him on the landing.

"Jeremiah! Hey!"

He couldn't help smiling at her, then realized he should probably make conversation. "So—who are you waiting for?" He hoped she wasn't there on a date. That would be awkward if some guy walked up to them. But Claire was looking at him with an odd expression on her face.

"You," she said after a couple of seconds.

"Me?" Jeremiah stared at her, wondering what he had missed.

Claire smiled nervously. "Didn't Porter tell you?"

Jeremiah shook his head slowly. What had his roommate done now?

Claire went on. "Well, he was tired, but he didn't want you to go alone. So he sent me instead."

Tired. Riiiiight. Dang that meddling man. Jeremiah was going to wring Porter's thick neck the next time he saw him. Still—it gave him an excuse to smell Claire's hair again. He took in a surreptitious sniff.

"Well, I guess you're cuter. . . ." he said lamely.

Claire blushed, then narrowed her big, brown eyes at him. Maybe she thought he was flirting with her. That made Jeremiah's face go hot too.

"I mean . . . no . . . yeah . . . well, you *are*." Jeremiah wanted to slap himself until his brain started functioning again.

Claire held up a dollar. "He even gave us money for a 'treat,'" she said with a giggle. She wore a watch on her up-held wrist, and she glanced at it. "We should find our seats."

"Have you seen *Macbeth* before?" Jeremiah asked at the same time. He stopped, waiting for her to finish speaking.

"No, sorry, you go ahead," Claire said.

Jeremiah grinned and offered his arm to her, and they went to look for their seats.

At the very top of the balcony, up against the lighting booth, Claire and Jeremiah stopped. *Typical Porter.* These had to be the cheapest tickets in the house. "I guess Porter got us good seats, huh?"

"Well, at least they're next to each other."

Jeremiah raised an eyebrow.

"I mean," she went on, "They could have been separated, right? Like, one could be down there, the other over here."

Jeremiah nodded. She was right. And after all, he wasn't really here to see the show, anyway. Porter had strong-armed him into a blind date of sorts, and that could be accomplished just as well from the back row as from the front.

They sat in silence as the people around them took their seats. As the house lights dimmed, Claire whispered, "So, I heard they're going to set this in Book of Mormon times."

Jeremiah rolled his eyes. *Honestly.* "Shakespeare?" he asked sarcastically. "And the Book of Mormon?"

"Yeah."

Jeremiah chortled. "What is it, like Macbeth meets Moroni and food storage?"

Claire didn't seem to appreciate his joke. "I think it's kind of cool." She frowned at him in the gathering dark. "Are you embarrassed about being Mormon?"

"No," he said. "I think the gospel should be part of everything we do. I just think telling Mormon stories makes us a target."

Claire seemed ready for a lively discussion on this topic. "Well, we have no problem with every other religion telling their stories," she said, leaning forward to make her point. The couple just in front of them turned around and gave them dirty glares. Claire sat back. Jeremiah could tell that she wasn't going to let the issue rest. He'd have to marshal his arguments during the show.

The stage lights came up. The set looked definitely Meso-American—it resembled some of the Mayan or Aztec temples Jeremiah had seen in photographs.

Despite his skepticism about the setting, Jeremiah found himself drawn into the dark plot of the play almost immediately. It all fascinated and terrified him at the same time. The way the witches put temptation into Macbeth's mind—which he harbored and let fester until it led to disaster, the subtle traps of pride and ambition, the way that ungodly revelation twisted and betrayed its receiver.

Most of all, Jeremiah felt Macbeth's horror at what he did. The stained dagger, the bloody hands. It was as if Jeremiah were reliving one of his nightmares of recent days. He wanted to punch Porter for making him come to this stupid show. It took everything he had to stay in his seat and not run screaming out into the night, shouting the details of his own dark deed to the rooftops.

It's nothing the same, he kept reminding himself as he gripped the armrests of his seat. But it *felt* the same.

• • •

As the house lights came up and the applause died down, Claire looked over at Jeremiah and got a shock. His face was white, and it looked like he was even trembling a little. Something about the play had disturbed him profoundly; he'd obviously been sucked into the story despite what he said earlier. Now he was staring off into space; Claire doubted that he knew she was there.

"Well," she said brightly, hoping to recapture his attention and lighten the mood a bit. "That's what I like—a nice, happy ending." She stared at Jeremiah, willing him out of his trance. He nodded, still lost in thought. Claire stood up. Maybe this date was a bad idea.

After she had taken a couple of steps down the row of seats, she heard Jeremiah following her. So he woke up after all. Claire shivered a bit. It was true that the dark mood of the play was hard to shake. She might have to chase its memory away with an episode of *The Cosby Show* when she got home so that she could get to sleep.

She and Jeremiah strolled slowly through the foyer, gazing at the pieces of student-created art mounted on the walls. The silence between them felt more comfortable now that Jeremiah seemed to be actually present. Claire tried again to start a conversation. Maybe she could get Jeremiah talking about why the play had freaked him out.

"That whole play just seemed so . . . unrealistic. Conspiracies can get so far-fetched." She chanced a glance at Jeremiah. He seemed to be paying attention this time. That gave her a little courage. "I mean, do you honestly believe that there are organizations nobody knows anything about that just want power and will do anything to get it?"

Jeremiah said nothing, but his eyes burned with intensity. Had she offended him? Her mother had always told her not to talk about politics on dates. As usual, she was right. Claire stopped and touched Jeremiah on the arm.

"No organization can be totally secret *and* totally evil," she said.

Jeremiah stared at the floor; it was as if he refused to meet her eyes.

"Hey. Miah?"

He seemed totally out of it again.

She waited until he noticed that the silence had grown awkward. Finally, he looked up at her, and she took his hand. He knew something he wasn't admitting; she could see it in his eyes. Then it hit her.

"You believe in them, don't you." It wasn't a question—it was a realization. Claire saw in an instant that she really didn't know very much at all about Jeremiah—that her affection for him was based mainly on what she'd assumed was his personality, his way of being. She saw now that there was a lot she needed to learn about him. She couldn't just think that she sensed goodness within him; she needed to know if it was there.

As if he read her thoughts, he let go of her hand and started walking. Claire kept up with him, a sudden chill descending upon her. Was Jeremiah involved in something dark and mysterious? Had the play brought up feelings of guilt? Suddenly, she didn't want to be alone with him anymore.

"Look," she said, not able to keep the agitation out of her voice. "I don't need to hear anything about this."

Jeremiah stopped walking and faced her. "I didn't, either, but . . ."

Claire shivered visibly and tried to keep moving. She wanted to go home now. But Jeremiah grabbed her arm.

"Look. What keeps them secret is the fact that nobody wants to believe they exist. And that's what they want."

Claire looked into his eyes and saw a stranger there. His grip hurt her arm. "Jeremiah, you're scaring me," she said, trying to make it sound like it was a joke, but it wasn't. He looked deadly serious, and so was she. She twisted out of his grasp, rubbing her arms to try to get rid of the chill. What if he was right? What if the secret combinations in the Book of Mormon had been revived in the latter days? Actually, that made sense, now that she thought about it. Weren't they prophesied to return?

"If they're so ruthless and powerful, then how can any of us be safe?" she wondered aloud.

"I don't know yet." Jeremiah was holding her coat; she'd forgotten about it. He put it around her shoulders with tenderness. Claire looked up at him as she put her arms into it. The stranger had gone, and all she saw was someone who was afraid, but who cared about her. He was vulnerable in this moment, sharing his fears so honestly. Claire wanted to honor that vulnerability and not do anything that would make Jeremiah retreat again. She took his arm and leaned against his shoulder, and they walked through the night.

After walking across campus through the clear, cold air, Claire felt much better. The oppression and shadows of the play had left them both, at least for the moment. She stopped on the top step of the porch that led into her building.

"Thanks for tonight," she said, smiling into his eyes. "Being with you was . . ." How could she describe it? Wonderful? Scary? Both?

Jeremiah laughed a little as she struggled to finish her sentence. "Yeah, me too."

Claire wanted to leave him knowing that she would try to understand his dark struggles. She wanted to build up his confidence in himself. He was a good man; she could feel it. Whatever it was he was fighting, he could win if he just had more confidence. More faith. And help from . . . friends who loved him.

"I felt safe," she confessed, even though it was only maybe 80 percent true. She could tell that her words meant something, touched him somehow. He leaned forward slightly, and it was as if there was a magnet pulling them toward one another. She closed her eyes, feeling his minty breath warm on her lips, waiting for him to kiss her, wanting it more than anything else right now.

The front door crashed open, and Jeremiah and Claire jumped apart. Two girls from the floor below Claire's eyed the two of them and giggled.

"Hey, Claire! Jeremiah?" Alison's sassy tone let Claire know that she was in for some serious teasing and interrogation later on.

"Anyway," Claire said, fighting the disappointment that their magic moment had been ruined.

"I had fun tonight," Jeremiah said.

"Thanks," Claire answered. Jeremiah seemed to be waiting for something, but Claire couldn't figure out what that might be.

After a moment, he nodded. "Well, good night."

"Oh!" Claire now guessed what Jeremiah's hesitation probably had been. "FHE! We still have to plan our lesson." Jeremiah's face went pale, and he looked embarrassed. *Oh.* She had guessed wrong. He'd forgotten all about it.

"I know you're busy," she said, hoping he wouldn't cancel on her—not after the evening they had just had. "So, I'll come early and just bring some stuff with me."

"Okay," Jeremiah said, but he avoided her eyes now. "That could work," he said, nodding. He walked off quickly, waving to her after a few steps, then turning and heading for his own dorm.

"Good night!" Claire called. She hated that he had to leave.

"Good night," he answered.

Something still nagged at her about the FHE conversation. "See you Monday?" For some reason, she needed to hear him say that he would be there.

"Yeah, Monday." She couldn't see his face, but he'd stopped and turned back toward her. She nodded and waved again. That would have to be enough.

EYES LIPS EYES LYRICS
(formerly known as Elizabethan Report)

🔊 **Send Ringtone to your Cell** 🔊

"Slept in Through Christmas"

I would've found a zeppelin
under the Christmas tree.
Could've carried me far across the sea
into the arms of my family.

I slept in through Christmas
oh oh oh oh
I slept in through Christmas
oh oh oh oh
Stayed up way too late

All the cars have turned to snow.
And now I think you would agree.
Let's spend the night below, below the mistle-
toe.
Santa walked in on me, me and my baby.

I slept in through Christmas
oh oh oh oh
I slept in through Christmas
aaaaaaah
I slept in through Christmas

Thanks to Miah for correcting these lyrics.

Submit Corrections   A-Z Lyrics

CHAPTER SIXTEEN

The Date

"Claire isn't my soul mate," Jeremiah insisted. He looked down at his shirt. It was buttoned crooked. Sighing, he started over. Porter, greatly resembling a plumber—in a really bad way—dug stuff out from under his bed. Jeremiah was half convinced that there was some sort of wormhole under Porter's bed, because how else could so much garbage fit under there? Old pizza boxes, dirty clothes, discarded pages of notebook paper with random scrawls on them—if Jeremiah hadn't been in such a hurry, he would have gone down to the maintenance closet, gotten a big black garbage bag, and chucked it all while Porter's head was still buried in the deeps.

"She won't be your soul mate if you bail on teaching Family Night with her. Especially to go out with that skank-muffin—ah ha!" Porter scooted himself out from under his bed and held his prize aloft—an old Nintendo, at least twenty years old. What the heck? Did that even still work?

"Look, Megan and I aren't going out on a date. She just had an extra ticket."

Porter assessed Jeremiah coolly, looking him up and down from where he knelt on their carpet. "Then why are you so dressed up?"

Whatever. Porter was too perceptive by half. Jeremiah grabbed his coat and slung it over his shoulder. "I just need a night off," he explained. Surely Porter—king of taking "personal days" from going to class—understood that. But no.

Porter's eyes showed judgment. "Some things you shouldn't take a night off from, Jay."

"Like FHE? It's every week. Seriously, can't you just cover for me?" He picked up his camera bag and walked to the door. He nodded at the Nintendo set. "You could teach an object lesson or something."

He left quickly before Porter had a chance to say anything else. He felt bad enough about this already. He hoped he was leaving early enough that he wouldn't run into Claire. He wouldn't be able to stand it if—

There she was, walking through the door with her arms full of lesson manuals and plastic-wrapped bowls. Of course she was early. Jeremiah stopped halfway down the last staircase then slunk back into the shadows as she passed into the Common Room. He hurried down the remaining steps so he could exit without getting caught. He was almost out when he heard footsteps behind him in the entryway.

"Jeremiah! Hey!" He turned. *Dangit.* He hated confrontation, and this one wasn't going to be pretty.

Claire didn't seem to notice that he wore his coat and was halfway out the door. She came forward excitedly. "Okay, so I was thinking that you could teach the faith and repentance part—I've got some quotes in here that you can use . . ." She pulled one of the manuals out of her pile and nearly dropped her entire armload.

"Oh, um. Actually, something came up. But Porter's going to cover for me," he said in a rush.

She dropped her gaze to the floor and opened and closed her mouth a couple of times. Then she cleared her throat and looked at him, brow furrowed. "Oh. Is everything okay? Is it an emergency?"

"Oh. Uh, no." Not exactly an emergency. Of course she was giving him the benefit of the doubt, which made him feel even worse for blowing her off like this. A voice inside, one that had been trying to get his attention all evening, spoke up again, but he squelched it firmly. "Everything's fine, so . . . good luck tonight. You'll be wonderful."

He ran out the door, feeling like the biggest jerk of all time.

He walked downtown to Penny Royal, the newest indie music club, psyching himself up for the concert as he went. It would be something he'd remember all his life. He'd loved this band since buying their first album—and the chance to go backstage? That didn't happen every day. When Elizabethan Report got really famous, he could tell people that he'd actually met them, back in the day. It was going to be a great night.

He arrived at the chic nightclub and gave his name to the hostess. She checked him off a list on a clipboard, after giving him a once-over. He walked in, the intense music of the warm-up band filling his ears. He looked around for Megan, but didn't see her. Had he made a mistake? This was where they were supposed to meet, wasn't it?

But then he saw her at the back of the room. She caught sight of him and was making her way through the crowd to greet him. She looked amazing. If Claire was a sweet, fresh flower, Megan resembled a polished crystal, gleaming and sparkling with energy. It was a good thing they were off campus; she wore a purple silk dress that looked modest enough to wear to the beach, but that was about it. She walked right up to him and stood a little closer than was polite.

"Ooh, Jeremiah. Hottest guy at the party, huh?" She winked as she crooned, and Jeremiah caught a whiff of dusky, exotic perfume.

"No, *you* are . . ." Except she wasn't a guy, idiot. "I mean . . . no you're not . . . Sorry." He should just leave now so he didn't cause himself any further embarrassment. Megan seemed to savor his discomfort, taking it as a compliment. Which he guessed it was, actually.

"So, uh," he said, practically yelling over the band, "When does Elizabethan Report start playing?" He thought he saw impatience flash in her eyes, but it was gone before he was sure.

"In just a little while," she assured him. "But come on," she said, ducking under his arm and moving in close. "I've got a surprise for you." She led him through the crowd the way she'd come. Jeremiah looked around at the place, decorated in the spare, hip fashion he associated with the East Coast. Exposed brick, vintage light fixtures, tastefully abstract art on the walls—it was as if he'd left the prosaic world of Provo far behind.

Megan stopped at a closed gate that rose up out of the floor. Looking beyond it, Jeremiah saw that it protected a staircase that went down to the basement level. A bouncer stood before it, dressed to the hilt, but looking painfully bored. He must have been imported from New York as well. Megan whispered in the bouncer's ear. He gave Jeremiah a measuring glance, then nodded and stepped aside.

She opened the gate and descended halfway into the darkness. She turned and flashed her million-dollar grin at Jeremiah. She beckoned him with the slightest tilt of her head, and he followed after her without speaking.

At the bottom of the stairs, Jeremiah stopped and looked around. If upstairs had been New York, this looked like something out of the grittiest, hippest part of Europe. Amsterdam, maybe, or Berlin. Lights flashed, and a DJ ground out hypnotic techno music. There weren't very many people down here; Jeremiah assumed it was some sort of private party. He looked around, hoping to recognize some band members. Maybe this was a greenroom.

Megan took his hands and walked backward into the depths of the basement. The music pumped even louder, and Jeremiah found it difficult to concentrate with the colored lights flashing in his eyes. A few people danced around him, but they all had their eyes closed as they bobbed up and down to the pervasive beat. Maybe Jeremiah should close his eyes, too; maybe that was the secret to surviving down here.

Jeremiah couldn't escape the growing warning feeling within him. He shouldn't be here. He knew he shouldn't ignore promptings; they'd always steered him to safety. But today during class and this evening while he was getting ready, he had pretended they weren't real, and had closed himself off to the guidance they provided. He regretted having been so bullheaded. What was wrong with him? He was still freaking out over the killing in the cave, but now he had to exercise faith. He'd been living out of fear the past few days, and darkness had grown thick around him.

Here, in this place, he felt that darkness all around. Strongly. He should leave.

Megan seemed to sense his discomfort. "Hey, don't be scared. So, do you want to know who your surprise is?"

"Surprise?" What could Megan possibly mean? What was she up to? Had she arranged to introduce him to the band herself? That would make all this worth it.

"Luc Dahl," she said in a rapturous tone.

Jeremiah stared at her blankly. "Who?" he asked after a minute. That wasn't the name of anyone in Elizabethan Report. Maybe he'd heard her wrong.

"Luc Dahl!" she shouted. The music was oppressively loud. Jeremiah wished desperately that they could go back upstairs. "Don't you know who that is?"

Jeremiah just shook his head.

"Look," she said, leaning right up close so he could feel how very thin the material of her tiny dress was. "I don't talk about it much, but when I was sixteen, my father had an accident at work. Mr. Dahl came in, and he paid for our house, my dad's physical therapy, he got me my job . . . *and he's paying for my tuition,*" she finished triumphantly.

Jeremiah looked away. Why was she telling him all this? What did it have to do with him? Megan put her hand on his shoulder and rubbed it gently.

"I don't know how you're doing financially," she went on. "But I can't imagine it's been easy."

Hah. Jeremiah shook his head. Since his parents' documents and papers had all burnt in the fire, Jeremiah's grandparents had a horrible time getting the insurance companies to make payments that were due to Jeremiah. There should be enough to cover his college and mission expenses at the very least—but Jeremiah had no idea when he'd see any of that money. In the meantime, he was glad his tuition and room and board were paid up through the end of the semester. He had almost no money for any extras, but he could survive if he had to.

"I've been worried about you," Megan said. "Mr. Dahl has been like a father to me. He can help you, too." She scanned the room, but didn't seem to find what she was looking for.

"But, hey. Come on." She pulled on his hand and leaned toward the middle of the dance floor, smiling at him seductively. He tried to hang back for a moment, but then gave in. She'd done a lot for him tonight, and he should be polite. What he really wanted to do was run upstairs, out the door, and back to FHE, but he followed her instead and began to dance.

They danced for a few minutes, Jeremiah trying to lose

his uncomfortable feelings in the relentless rhythm of the music, but it only made him more agitated. Maybe he just wasn't used to places like this—maybe that was what was making him uncomfortable. He needed to get out in the world more and stop being so sensitive. He consciously shoved back at the warning whispers in his mind until they retreated. Finally, a voice broke the discomfort of the moment.

"Megan?"

Jeremiah opened his eyes. That was weird; he didn't remember closing them. The music. It was getting to him, shutting down his senses somehow. This place—what was it about it? He looked over Megan's shoulder and saw a man striding toward them. She turned, squealed, and ran to the man, giving him a huge hug as they met.

"Hello, sweetheart," he said warmly to her. They clearly knew each other very well. He wasn't tall, but looked substantial. He was older—maybe fifty—but he and Megan would make a handsome couple that people wouldn't even blink at, except in admiration, in Hollywood or on Madison Avenue.

The main impression he gave off was of substantial wealth. From his immaculate grooming to his camelhair jacket over a cashmere turtleneck and subtle designer jeans—this was a man used to getting what he wanted. He turned to Jeremiah and smiled, revealing impeccable dental work.

"Are you Jeremiah?" he asked.

"Yeah," said Jeremiah shyly, suddenly conscious of the

fact that his sport jacket probably needed to visit the dry cleaner's.

The man didn't feel the need to introduce himself, probably assuming that everyone here already knew who he was.

"Megan told me about your situation," the man said, concern emanating from his tanned face. "I am so sorry. My parents died when I was seventeen. I had just registered for college." He leaned forward as if he were going to share a secret. "The funeral is tough. But what happens afterward is even worse. Everybody returns to their lives, and you're left all alone."

Jeremiah nodded. Finally, someone understood. That was exactly right.

The man went on. "Fortunately, a Mr. Gainsborough read about my story in the newspaper. He practically adopted me. He showed me there was a better way. I want to return that favor by giving someone else a once-in-a-lifetime opportunity. I've chosen you, Jeremiah."

He clapped his hand on Jeremiah's shoulder. "I want to offer you a job. Five thousand dollars a month, plus your apartment, food, and tuition. Part-time, mostly, but on-call when I need you. Are you available?"

Jeremiah realized that his mouth was hanging open. Five thousand dollars a month for part-time work? And most of his expenses already paid? What would he do with all of that money?

His mind quickly gave him answers. Buy a freaking car, for one thing. Hire a private investigator to look into the circumstances of his parents' deaths. Take Claire to a nice restaurant—maybe lots of nice restaurants. Claire would have to be impressed by that.

"Yeah, yeah," he said with enthusiasm. Then he remembered. "I mean, until my mission."

Mr. Dahl looked at him with a raised, perfectly manicured eyebrow. "Mission?"

"I'm serving a mission for my church in May," Jeremiah explained. *Dumb.* He had assumed that Mr. Dahl was LDS. Even if he wasn't, he had to know what a mission was.

"Oh," said Mr. Dahl, seeming to reconsider. "I hoped I'd be able to use you a little longer than that." The look on his face made it clear that Jeremiah's mission changed everything. "Don't worry. We can certainly talk about it when you get back. Keep in touch?" He handed Jeremiah an engraved business card and turned away. Jeremiah had been dismissed.

Megan looked a little panicked. "Mr. Dahl, what kind of time commitment are you thinking?"

The man turned back and gave it a moment's thought. "Six months," he said. Then, as if an idea had just occurred to him, "Could you delay your mission that long, Jeremiah? I'd like to repay Mr. Gainsborough."

Jeremiah smiled, unable to believe his good fortune. He'd planned on putting his mission papers in so he could go into the MTC the minute he turned nineteen in May, but he could wait six months—take a few more classes during spring and summer terms, even, so he'd be that much further ahead when he got home.

Mr. Dahl's phone rang. He pulled it out of his pocket and checked the screen. "Excuse me," he said formally. "Think about it for just a minute. I need to take this call."

"I don't really need time to think about it," Jeremiah blurted out. "I'll take it."

Mr. Dahl gave him a perfunctory smile, nodded, and stepped away as he turned his attention to his phone.

Megan turned to Jeremiah with stars in her eyes. She pressed herself up against him with excitement. "Can you believe it? Mr. Dahl! As in Gainsborough-Dahl Transglobal?"

Jeremiah was still stunned. Of course he'd heard of GDT; it was one of the largest conglomerates in the world. He just hadn't connected Mr. Dahl's name with it. This was an incredible opportunity.

Megan was practically hopping up and down on her stilettos with excitement. "You've got it made," she squealed, cozying up even closer to him. "*We've* got it made."

We? Jeremiah looked down at her, and it was as if someone had thrown a bucket of ice water in his face. He barely knew her—and here she was, luring him with a job offer that sounded way too good to be true. Something had to be wrong here.

Yes.

Something was very wrong. Jeremiah turned his attention inward, truly listening for the first time all day. He wasn't supposed to be here. He wasn't supposed to be with Megan. Suddenly, Claire's face appeared in his mind as clearly as if he were seeing it on a movie screen.

Claire wouldn't care whether he had a car or money to take her to fancy restaurants. She certainly wouldn't care where he worked, or whether he was the "hottest boy in the club." Everything that Megan had held up as desirable in the past half hour—Jeremiah could see now that he wanted none of it.

The music pumped into a deafening crescendo, and the room seemed full of sinister presences. He had to get out of here. He felt like he was going to suffocate.

Jeremiah turned to Megan and handed her Mr. Dahl's business card.

Megan stared at him suspiciously. "Jeremiah," she began.

Jeremiah cut her off before she could try to persuade him to stay. He didn't trust himself right now, and he felt like his hold on the Spirit was tenuous at best. He had to obey this prompting if he hoped to receive another.

"I'm sorry. I need to go. I just remembered I need to help Claire with FHE."

Megan's face darkened with anger and disbelief. "You've got to be kidding me. Luc Dahl is Bill Gates— times five."

That didn't matter. None of it mattered. Jeremiah started walking backward to the staircase that would lead him out of this crazy place. "Look, I shouldn't have come. If I hurry, I can still make it."

"To FHE?" Suddenly, in her derision, Megan was much less attractive. She made one last plea. "Hey, just wait until Mr. Dahl gets back."

He shrugged his shoulders apologetically, then turned and went up the stairs as fast as he could. At the top, he had the fleeting satisfaction of momentarily displacing the bouncer's look of perpetual ennui. He hurried past the man and looked around, trying to figure out which direction was the quickest way out.

The front of the club was filling rapidly with adoring Elizabethan Report fans, so Jeremiah chose the back exit sign that seemed to lead past the bathrooms. He hurried down a dim hallway to a metal door. Would an alarm go off if he went out this way? He decided to chance it, desperate to get back to Claire and keep his promise to her.

He pushed it open and found himself in a dank alleyway. Immediately he had the cold sensation that unfriendly eyes were upon him. He ran toward the main street, then turned the corner and walked rapidly up the sidewalk. After just a few yards, he heard footsteps behind him. He looked over his shoulder; a man walked just behind him, obviously intent on stopping him. He hadn't seen his face, but Jeremiah was suddenly sure that it was Magus. Who was he? Mr. Dahl's henchman? A partner of the man he'd killed in the cave?

Jeremiah broke into a run, but Magus caught up to him almost immediately, and two more men seemed to come out of nowhere. One pinned his arms behind his back, while the other shoved a dark hood over his head. Jeremiah heard a car screech to a halt next to them, and the next thing he knew, he was shoved roughly into the back seat and sandwiched between the two hulking men.

The car took off, Jeremiah's forehead slamming into

the seat behind him as it did so. It appeared that these people didn't believe in seatbelts. But that was the least of Jeremiah's problems at the moment.

• • •

At the front door of the club, Megan shivered in her skimpy dress. She watched the dark sedan speed around the corner and into the night. What had gone wrong? Jeremiah had seemed so excited about working for Mr. Dahl, but when he had changed his mind, he must have made someone angry.

She didn't like being out of the loop about what was going on. More was happening here than she'd bargained for, more than she felt was appropriate for the situation. She had to get Brenna on the phone immediately. She pulled her earpiece out of her evening bag, speed dialed Brenna's number, and stalked back into the noisy club. This had not gone the way she had thought it would, but she could still fix this. She had to.

CHAPTER SEVENTEEN

The Break

Megan stared at her phone, mesmerized by the feed from Brian's secret camera. *Thank heaven for that geek,* she thought. This was priceless access—but Megan grew horrified as she kept watching.

Someone had removed the hood over Jeremiah's head, and now a man stepped in front of him, yelling and mocking. The camera didn't have audio, but it was evidently not a pleasant conversation.

Then it got much worse, the man repeatedly hitting and kicking Jeremiah, who had to be tied to something. Megan flinched with each blow. The violence sickened her; this was her fault. Megan had set him up. Jeremiah had trusted her, and now he was being beaten to a pulp.

Megan watched with growing alarm and dialed Brenna's number again. She ran to get her coat as she waited for the call to go through.

Yes. Brenna picked up this time.

She explained what had happened, but Brenna seemed curiously unfazed by the whole thing. Had she known that this was going to happen? Megan rushed to her car and drove to the dark Zooby News offices. She swiped her key-card through the access point and made straight for Brenna's office, walking as quickly as she could in her heels.

Brenna was on the phone with someone else, calmly commenting once in a while as if nothing in the world was wrong.

Megan waited as patiently as she could, getting her breath back and trying to calm herself. She couldn't help but listen in on Brenna's side of the conversation. "They won't show any mercy. People don't just disappear." Somehow, Megan was sure that Brenna was not working on a breaking story in some revolution-torn, third-world country.

Brenna clicked off her headset and turned her attention to Megan.

"Brenna!" Megan said, trying to keep her voice from climbing up an octave in her fright. "Jeremiah's being tortured." For some reason, that made Megan dissolve into tears like a ninny. *Get it together, Halling.* She had to be strong—assertive and confident, like her mentor.

Brenna once again seemed unsurprised. "Have you seen him?" she asked calmly.

"No, but I had his friend Brian plant a spy camera on his coat, and I saw the video feed."

Brenna grew even more still and alert. This was some-how important, Megan sensed. She wondered if she could use it to her advantage somehow. "Has anyone else seen it?" Brenna asked quietly.

"Only me. We have to call the police."

Brenna half smiled. "We are not calling the police, Megan."

What? This was going beyond the journalistic need to be ahead of the story; this was blatant disregard for what was happening to an innocent man.

"They could kill him!" she cried. "I'm calling the police." She opened her evening bag and dug her phone out of the bottom.

Brenna stopped her cold with a single sentence. "The only reason we have Jeremiah is because of you—remember?"

We? Megan was confused. Brenna hadn't said that the men who wanted to question Jeremiah had anything to do with Zooby News. Fear nearly closed her throat, but she spoke through clenched teeth. "You said they wanted to *talk* to him. You didn't say they were going to hurt him. That's wrong."

Brenna looked impatient with her, as if she were a child. "You have no idea what's in that box and what it can do." She paused and switched to a more persuasive tone. "We work for the good guys. They'd never ask us to do anything that's wrong . . . or unnecessary."

That last rationalization was not lost on Megan. Realizing that she was turning her back on a once-in-a-lifetime career opportunity, she took out the earpiece and set it on Brenna's desk. It was the school's property, and she wanted no part of it now. She turned to leave. She'd go somewhere else to get help for Jeremiah. She'd call Mr. Dahl as soon as she got back to her car.

Once again, Brenna's casually dropped words stopped her—this time at the door. "So—what would you like me to do with that voicemail saying you convinced Jeremiah to go to the concert—that you had him *ready* for us . . ."

Megan stopped and turned back. Then she realized what Brenna was threatening. Blackmail, pure and simple. Brenna would turn around and pin responsibility for this on her? *Unbelievable.* Mr. Dahl wouldn't stand for this. Would he? All the evidence pointed to her and to her alone. Brenna seemed to have no qualms about throwing her "protégée" under the bus, if need be.

Megan had really painted herself into a corner in the name of advancing her budding career. She'd thought she was so savvy, but now she saw how naive she must have appeared to everyone around her. She mentally kicked herself for her stupidity.

Brenna got up from her desk and moved around it, holding out her hands. "Megan, you are the most talented student I've ever had. With the right opportunity, you'll go straight to the top. And I've never seen a more perfect opportunity than this one."

She picked up Megan's earpiece off the desk and held it out. "Come on," she urged softly. "You've got a story to tell the world."

Push or pull; carrot or stick? Brenna had her either way. Megan hated feeling trapped like this, but she couldn't see a way out for the moment. She had to evaluate what this meant for her future—what it meant for her father's future. There was so much at stake, and she was too stressed out right now to sort it all out. She needed some space so that she could get some clarity on the situation. She decided that she'd better play nice, at least for the moment. It would give her time to figure out what her next move should be. She took the earpiece back, staring sullenly at Brenna the whole time.

"Good girl." Brenna beamed at her. For the first time, Megan regretted ever having taken the job that Mr. Dahl had so generously offered her. That GDT youth group flyer she had picked up in high school—for so long, she had thought it was an answer to prayers, but now she wondered whether it had been a vicious trap. She smiled, just to give Brenna the illusion of acquiescence, and left the dark building.

QUOTATION FOUND ON CALBERT DAVENPORT'S BULLETIN BOARD IN HIS OFFICE AT THE FENIMORE PARETO INSTITUTE FOR ECONOMIC POLICY.

G THE SAINTS, ETC.   79

year,	and in the work of God? No, the
can	providences of God are all a miracle
must	to the human family until they
can	understand them. There are no
turn	miracles only to those who are
ents	ignorant. A miracle is supposed to
our	be a result without a cause, but there
the	is no such thing. There is a cause
ish to	for every result we see; and if we see
ed to	a result without understanding the
the	cause we call it a miracle. This is
not	what we have been taught; but there
co-	is no miracle to those who understand.

her Carrington was
pounds

CHAPTER EIGHTEEN

Interrogation

Jeremiah flinched and screwed his eyes shut as one of his captors pulled the hood off his head. He opened his eyes gradually as they adjusted to the light. Magus, the man who'd chased him through the parking garage, stood over him, holding a gun.

Jeremiah struggled against his bonds. His abductors had tied both his arms and legs to a metal chair, and his movements threatened to topple the rickety thing onto the concrete floor. He looked up at his captor.

Magus had a sardonic smile on his lean, wolfish face. "Are you ready to get rid of the box? Hasn't it caused you enough trouble?"

Jeremiah examined his assailant's face carefully. This was not the person who had orchestrated the attacks on him; he must work for someone else. He was here with Jeremiah in this dank, cold room, while whoever pulled the strings watched from a safe distance. Jeremiah scanned the ceiling for cameras, but saw none. That didn't mean they weren't there.

Magus walked around Jeremiah slowly, stopping when he reached Jeremiah's right side. He stuck his gun in the back of his belt and grabbed the camera bag from Jeremiah's shoulder. He took out the video camera, hefting it so he could examine its controls in the bad light. He pressed the play button, and the video of Jeremiah's parents started rolling.

The man chuckled. "Did I tell you I met them once?" He paused the film and pressed fast forward. "I was driving a semitruck," he said idly, watching Jeremiah's reaction out of the corner of his eye.

Jeremiah's heart raged. He wished he could break the bonds that held him and throttle the monster standing in front of him. But he sat motionless. Was this some kind of a test? He didn't say anything. Magus pressed play again and watched the screen carefully.

"Who is this?" He held the camera before Jeremiah's eyes. It was the film of Jeremiah and Ammon entering the cave in Manti. The camera panned the small room, taking in the scrolls, the swords, and the box on its central pillar.

"Where is this?" he asked.

"I don't know," Jeremiah said.

Quick as lightning, Magus turned and struck him across the face. Jeremiah reeled with the impact, and the chair nearly fell over.

"Tell me where the cave is," Magus instructed with false patience.

Jeremiah shook his head. Magus hit him again. Hard. Not with anger, just because he could.

Then Magus grabbed him by the neck and held him close as he scanned through the rest of the video footage.

• • •

Porter stood in front of the Common Room TV. Two of the guys from his floor sat before it, his vintage Nintendo controllers in their hands. The rest of the Family Home Evening group sat around watching with various degrees of attention. Some slept openly; others yawned covertly and kept glancing over at the refreshment table. Brian, Simon, and Lilah were giving him their full focus, though. He was grateful for that.

"And thus we see that Super Mario wears his boots and overalls even while swimming . . ." He paused and smiled at his awesome girlfriend, whose eyes twinkled in return. "I think this demonstrates the very important point of dressing modestly even while at the pool." He looked around. It was time to stop; he should quit while he was ahead. "I guess Claire never came back, so I think we should go ahead and eat the Rice Krispie treats she brought."

Everyone stood quickly—even the two guys who had been snoring in the corner—and descended like locusts upon the refreshments. It was difficult to believe that they'd eaten dinner just an hour or two before. Lilah ignored the Rice Krispie treats and came straight over to Porter. She loved him even better than dessert, and that meant everything to Porter. She hugged him, then froze, looking over his shoulder. He turned so he could see what she was looking at.

That tramp Megan stood in the doorway in the tiniest dress Porter had ever seen. She was the one that needed the lesson Porter had just taught. How was that even legal? She'd better not get caught by the Standards department. *Or maybe she should,* Porter thought slyly. He wondered whether he could make an anonymous report.

Besides the sleazy dress, she looked awful; there was a tear in her nylons, she was shivering—how could she not be freezing when she was practically naked—and mascara ran down her overly made-up face.

"Well, look what the cat dragged in," Porter said, losing the feeling of expansive charity he'd felt while teaching his FHE object lesson. Lilah smacked him on the arm and rushed over to Trampasaurus Rex.

"Megan, are you okay? What happened?" That was so like Lilah. She saw the good in everybody, even when it didn't exist. A flash of insight came to Porter. He had to be grateful for Lilah's extraordinary vision, because that gift was one of the reasons she put up with him. She saw the good in him even when it was buried deep. He couldn't begrudge her doing the same for anyone else.

Megan started crying. Porter didn't have Lilah's compassion, and had trouble believing Megan's tears were anything more than a bid for attention. What did she want, anyway? After a few minutes, she visibly pulled herself together and walked over to him.

"Porter, I have to ask you a favor."

Porter set his jaw. *Let's nip this in the bud, shall we?* "The answer is no."

Lilah gave him a quick glare. "He means yes," she said gently. "What do you need?"

"I'm really scared," Megan said, her voice trembling. "I need help."

This was nuts. He'd call her bluff. "What did you do, ditch my roommate at SkankFest?"

Megan froze and seemed to crumple in on herself. Lilah gave him a stern look, and Porter knew he was treading on thin ice.

"Never mind," Megan mumbled. "I'll take care of it."

"Are you sure?" asked Lilah. "We're happy to help."

Megan shook her head and pulled away. Lilah followed after her. "Megan! At least let me give you a ride. It's cold outside." Megan turned, then smiled gratefully through her raccoon eyes. Lilah ran back to Porter, gave him a quick peck on the cheek, then followed Megan out the door.

Whatever.

A few feet away, Brian stared after Megan. How much of their conversation had he overheard? Porter cleared his throat, and Brian looked up at him guiltily. *Great.* Brian had the hots for Megan. *Another one bites the dust.* Porter decided his next Family Home Evening lesson was going to be about choosing appropriate women. He mused on that. He could probably find some quotes from Grandpa Rockwell's journal that would apply to the situation.

• • •

Magus had his hand firmly around Jeremiah's neck, forcing him to watch the footage from the cave yet again. "You don't have to give an answer—but we had you followed. So, just exactly where in Manti is this cave?"

On screen, Jeremiah raised the sword and thrust it into the assassin's chest.

Magus laughed with what sounded like genuine surprise and pleasure. "You're a murderer, Jeremiah." He made it sound like he was welcoming him to an exclusive club.

Jeremiah pushed down the now-familiar surge of guilt. "Whatever the Lord requires is right," he insisted, as much for his own benefit as that of his captors.

Magus looked at him in mock shock. "Who do you think you are that God would tell you to do that?" He indicated the video screen; he froze it on the exact frame in which Jeremiah plunged the sword into the man's heart. "You weren't listening to God. You were listening to somebody else. Where's the box?" he added, almost as an afterthought. He was probably trying to trick Jeremiah into a confession.

Magus waited for a few seconds, then pulled a gun out and aimed it at Jeremiah. Jeremiah stared at him, mentally daring him to get on with it. They gazed into each other's eyes for a few more seconds.

Finally, Jeremiah lost patience. "Do it!" he shouted desperately. "What's the problem? Do it, then! If you're going to shoot me, shoot me!" He stared at Magus, realization dawning. He grinned, his bruised cheeks smarting with the effort. "You can't. Because you need me. And you need the box. You won't kill me."

Magus smiled and cocked his head, as if he was giving Jeremiah points. He walked over to the steel door in the corner and banged on it a few times. It opened almost immediately, and Jeremiah was stunned to see Claire shoved roughly into the room. Her hands were tied in front of her, and she was gagged with a dirty rag. She ran to Jeremiah's side and stared at him, pleading with her eyes.

"Claire!" Jeremiah cried, rage and fear flooding through him again. He looked at Magus. "She has nothing to do with this."

She leaned close to Jeremiah, shivering as she had on their date. Her face was deathly pale in the flickering light. Jeremiah felt sick with guilt that she had been dragged into this mess.

Magus held up the camera again and pressed Play, holding the screen so Claire could see what was happening on screen.

"Claire," moaned Jeremiah. "Don't watch that." But it was too late.

"When she sees who you really are, she won't want you." Magus said smugly.

Claire flinched as she watched the replay of Jeremiah stabbing the man in the cave. Jeremiah watched her face, stricken that she had to witness the killing. It was bad enough that it was seared onto his brain; now she'd never be able to forget it either. When it came to that last, awful frame, she jumped in shock. She looked at Jeremiah, tears spilling down her lovely face. In agony, Jeremiah closed his eyes momentarily. Magus knew what he was doing. This was much worse than the physical beatings. Much, much worse.

Magus flipped off the camera and held up the gun. Pointing it straight at Claire's head and ostentatiously flipping off the safety, he looked at Jeremiah. "The box or her, Jeremiah."

Jeremiah shook his head, terrified that he was being asked to make this choice. He'd made a solemn promise that he would never reveal the box's location, but when he made that vow, he never expected to be forced to act upon it. It was unreasonable; this was far too much to ask under the circumstances. No box was worth an innocent life.

"No!" he cried. "Just—look, put the gun down, okay? I'll tell you."

Magus leaned toward Jeremiah, waiting. Jeremiah looked at Claire's tear-streaked face. He bowed his head and prayed.

A moment later, it hit him. No. He could not break his promise. He thought of Joseph Smith; he thought of Nephi. God had asked them both to do hard things, and they had come through with faith and obedience. Why should he be held to a lower standard?

No matter how painful it was, he had to keep his word. He had to exercise faith that God loved him and had his best interests at heart. He had to trust that whatever happened would be what was right. The Spirit rose up within him, confirming that keeping his promise was the correct decision. He opened his eyes and swallowed hard around the lump in this throat. Heart thudding in his chest, he looked up at

Claire again. He'd started to hope that she might be someone he could love and grow old with, someone who could be his best friend the way his parents had been best friends. Now it looked like that was not to be. And that crushed him.

"Claire, I don't know how to say this, but I promised. I can't tell, no matter what. I'm so sorry."

Claire looked at him with panic in her eyes, but as she gazed at him, she suddenly relaxed as if she understood. Jeremiah prayed that the Spirit was also with her, whispering comfort to her heart as well. She nodded; she knew. Jeremiah turned his head and glared at his torturer.

"Tell me where the box is," Magus said.

"No." Jeremiah spoke the word firmly, but with utter peace in his heart.

Not hesitating, Magus aimed the gun and fired it directly at Claire's head.

•   •   •

Magus looked around the room, his ears ringing with the deafening report of the pistol. A bright, white light had flashed at exactly the same moment as he fired the gun, momentarily blinding him. Now, with green spots before his eyes, he looked wildly around the room. Impossible. Jeremiah and his girlfriend were gone. They'd disappeared from a locked room. He glanced up at the hidden surveillance camera, hoping that the man watching on the other end had a better clue as to what just happened than he did.

Swearing long and creatively, he kicked over the metal

chair. It skittered across the concrete floor until it crashed into the opposite wall. Success had been within his grasp; he'd been so close.

And now—Magus knew his own life was in jeopardy. There was nothing for it, but he dreaded walking out of this prison into the room beyond. He was going to pay for the escape of those two, and pay dearly. He might have a slight chance of redeeming himself and going after Jeremiah once more, but he doubted it. He doubted it very much.

☐ Sort by ▾

☐ ✉ Re: Comparative Symbology
☐ ✉ Re: LARP tournament! Take down the Dark Elves!!!
☐ ✉ The Ark in America - what historians don't want you to know...

83 messages

Reply Reply all Forward

Re: Comparative Symbology

From: Mail Delivery Subsystem <mailer-daemon@trillomail.com>
Sent: Mon, Sept. 17, 2007
To: trustno1.brian@trillomail.com

Delivery to the following recipient failed permanently:

    cdavenport@fenimorepareto.org

Technical details of permanent failure:
DNS Error: Domain name not found

----- Original message -----

Subject: Re: Comparative Symbology
From: Brian Bateman <trustno1.brian@trillomail.com>
To: cdavenport@fenimorepareto.org
Content-Type: BASE64: RHIuIEQuIFlvdXIgbGlmZSBpcyBpbiBkYW5nZXI=

Dear Professor Davenport,

I just finished your essay on the Navajo code talkers, and I wanted to let you know what a big fan I am of your work. I was wondering whether you would reconsider your decision not to make public speeches anymore. I am the president of my local chapter of CombinationsRevealed.org, and I know your work would find a warm reception in my hometown.

I wondered, too, whether you had changed your position on the Illuminati-Templar connection after reading the paper Dr. Bosworth presented at Cambridge last summer. I found the salient points of his case for a post-Enlightenment revival quite convincing.

Anyway, please let me know if you'd be willing to come speak to our group.

Sincerely,

Brian B. Bateman

DATE: 17 SEPTEMBER 2007
DESC.: C. DAVENPORT EMAIL
EVIDENCE FILE #: 3.10.6.22

NOTES:
EMAIL BOUNCED FROM CALBERT DAVENPORT'S CLOSED ACCOUNT;
ORIGINALLY SENT 09/17/12.

ple on that very

nti? (For thos

found directly in back of the Temple in Manti City. Some say
and others think that the top portion is original, but the lower

CHAPTER NINETEEN

Friends and Family

Lilah covered her mouth so that Porter wouldn't hear her sigh of frustration over the phone. She loved him dearly, but sometimes he was a human wrecking ball.

"You really hurt Megan's feelings, sweetie," she said. "I think she's trying to change, but it's not very motivating to do that when people keep judging you and forcing you back into a pigeonhole."

"Sorry," Porter said. "But no one else put Megan in her place. I had to." He paused. Lilah could hear him huffing a little; he must be going up the dorm stairs toward his room. She had to get him going to the gym again. "Okay, maybe FHE wasn't the best place to do it, but it didn't ruin Claire's treats for anybody . . . Jeremiah!"

Lilah jerked the phone away from her ear as Porter bellowed his friend's name.

"He's not here," Porter said, and Lilah put the phone back to her ear. "That's weird. Hey, let me call you back."

Lilah waited up for another hour, passing the time

reading, but Porter never called back. No matter, she thought, as she turned out the lights. She'd see him in the morning.

The next day, Lilah sneaked into the men's dorm and headed upstairs to Porter's room. She'd gotten her mail earlier, and Jeremiah's test results had arrived. She had opened the envelope out of habit—then once it was open, decided there wasn't any harm in looking at the results. She knew Porter and Jeremiah wanted to treat this as a huge secret— hence her flouting all the rules and coming up here to the Forbidden Zone. Well, she'd wake them both up and give them the news.

It was sad that Porter lived in the freshman dorm at his age, but she couldn't deny the practicality of it. It was the cheapest housing available, and he did qualify for it, credit-wise. Lilah wondered whether next semester he could get his own apartment, though.

Was it too much to hope for that they might meet the requirements for married student housing at that point? Lilah tried not to let herself daydream. She and Porter had been dating for four years. Her friends kept telling her that she should move on.

But every time she contemplated breaking up with him—which she realized was the logical thing to do—a voice inside her urged her to stay. It didn't feel like a desperate, "you're an old maid—you'll never find another man" voice, either. It was calm, peaceful, and patient. She leaned on the memory of that voice when it seemed that she and

Porter were destined to hold hands and kiss each other good-bye at curfew for the rest of eternity.

She knocked softly on Porter's door. When no one answered, she went in quietly and closed the door behind her. It looked like Jeremiah was already up and gone. That was disappointing; she'd looked forward to his reaction to the news about his heritage. Porter was snoring so loudly that Lilah was surprised the window blinds weren't rattling. That would take some getting used to, assuming they ever got married. She filed that away for further contemplation and tiptoed to his side.

"Sweetie," she whispered.

Porter sprang up from his mattress and pointed a finger gun at her.

"Freeze," he yelled, bleary-eyed and blinking.

"Porter!" Lilah said firmly. She raised her eyebrows at him as he came to full consciousness. He focused on her after a moment and wiped his brow. He leaned back and sighed.

"Don't scare me like that," he said.

Lilah held up the envelope. "I've got Jeremiah's DNA test results."

"Ah! You didn't open it, did you?" he said, looking aghast.

"It was addressed to me," Lilah said, trying not to sound defensive.

"Only to protect him from British assassins." He grabbed the envelope from her. "What does it say?" he asked, peering into the open end.

"It says his maternal line is from Guatemala."

Porter frowned. "And his paternal?"

"There was some kind of error, and they were unable to trace his paternal line. Says they need a new saliva sample. So where is he?"

Porter looked over at Jeremiah's bed. It was still made.

"He must not have come home from his night on the town with the Queen of Harpies." Lilah shook her head at Porter's harsh criticism of Megan, but Porter wasn't paying attention. He swung his legs over the side of the bed. "Something's wrong. It's not like Jay to be gone this long without any word. This can't be good."

The door flew open, and Lilah jumped up in shock. Porter could get kicked out of school—again—if anyone knew she was here. It didn't look good at all. But the person at the door was only Brian, who stormed in and walked over to Jeremiah's headboard. He reached under the top shelf and pulled something out from under it. He turned and held it up. "I think this could lead us to Jeremiah," he said.

Noting Brian's dramatic flair, Lilah glanced at Porter. He really needed to fill her in on what was going on.

Porter glared at Brian, suspicion all over his face. "How did you find that?" he asked as he snatched it away.

Brian shrugged. "It's obvious," he said in his unconsciously condescending way. "I saw it from the hall."

Lilah looked at the note over Porter's shoulder. It was classy-looking—square, handmade paper with letterpress writing and calligraphy. But what did the words mean?

"Manti Road, Mile Marker 3." Why would someone have a party out there?

Simon popped his head in the door, holding some space-age-looking contraption connected to an MP3 player. He smiled eagerly at Brian. "Did you know that your iPod can hear everything that's going on in this room?" he asked, loud enough for the whole floor to hear. Brian snatched the contraption out of his roommate's hands and tried to fake astonishment, but Lilah wasn't fooled. The device explained a lot.

Brian spoke quickly, as if trying to deflect the focus away from him. "I think we should go to Manti."

Porter considered for a moment, then nodded.

"And I think we should take Megan, because she might know something," Brian added hesitantly.

Porter started to object, but Lilah took his arm and squeezed it in one of their secret codes. He relaxed, and she patted him with approval.

"I agree with Brian," she said. "She could use some friends and a nice drive. I'll call her. I was really worried about her last night."

Porter clearly didn't like the sound of that, but he said nothing. *Atta boy.* He was learning.

Lilah called Megan, who didn't take much convincing. She said she'd meet them outside in fifteen minutes.

When it was time to go, Porter sent Simon and Brian out first so they could make sure the coast was clear for Lilah's exit. The two boys waited for Lilah and Porter in the back entryway, then shot out the door toward Lilah's car.

"Shotgun! I've got shotgun!" Simon and Brian both yelled as they raced. Lilah laughed. Porter could be immature at times, but next to his friends, he often looked as wise and venerable as King Benjamin. Neither of Porter's neighbors seemed to realize that they'd be riding in back, since of course Porter got shotgun automatically.

Lilah unlocked the car just as Megan walked up. She stood next to the car awkwardly. Lilah ran over and hugged her. Why couldn't Porter see how lost and alone she was? *All ugliness is born of pain*, she reminded herself, and made a mental note to share that nugget of truth with Porter later.

She turned and motioned for Porter to come over. He obeyed, not quite dragging his feet. Lilah frowned; he was skating on thin ice again. He caught her look and instantly turned on meekness.

"Hey, Megan," he mumbled, scuffing the asphalt with the toe of his boot. Lilah narrowed her eyes, willing him to apologize. He got her brainwave and looked Megan in the eye. "Hey, I'm really sorry about last night. I was really worried about Jeremiah. And Claire."

Megan's face went even paler than it normally was. "Claire? What about her?"

"She left FHE when she got a text and didn't come back. We had to eat the Rice Krispie treats without her."

Megan looked up at the mountains that loomed above the campus, naked fear on her face. She looked like she might faint. Porter reached for her arm. "You okay?"

"Yeah." Megan nodded vigorously and flashed her million-dollar smile.

Whoa, girl. Lilah knew that for Megan, flirting was probably instinctive, but Lilah didn't want the girl getting any ideas. She tried to herd them back to the task at hand. "We're going to find everybody. Come on."

Lilah unlocked the car doors, and Brian and Simon jostled one another as they tried to get in the front seat. Porter walked over to where they stood and waited for their attention. Brian and Simon still didn't seem to get that they didn't have eminent domain. Lilah thought of a way to break the impasse.

"How about if Megan sits in the middle?" she suggested.

Brian and Simon looked at Lilah, then over at Megan. They broke for the back doors and tried to get the other to get in first. Megan stood there, but didn't get in.

"Come on, Megan. Let's go!" said Porter, but she took a step backward.

"You okay?" Lilah asked. She wondered what was spooking the poor thing. The boys were as boisterous as puppies, but they were harmless. Surely Megan could see that.

Megan smiled—not her runway model smile, but one full of sadness and regret. "You guys just go on without me."

"You sure?" asked Porter.

Megan nodded, not looking anyone in the face. "Yeah, it's a long drive. You'll need the room."

Lilah noted dryly that both Brian and Simon looked as if they'd received news that a childhood pet had just been flattened by a steamroller.

Porter was doing his best to look concerned, not relieved. "Okay," he said. He glared at the other guys until they got into the backseat, as docile as lambs.

Lilah looked back at Megan one more time and resolved to call her to check on her once they got down to Manti. She got in the car, started it, and they were off.

• • •

Megan watched Lilah's yellow SUV pull out of the student parking lot, then pulled her phone's earpiece out of her pocket. The phone was already buzzing; she put the earpiece in her ear and braced herself for what was to come.

"Hello?" she said. "No, I didn't get to them in time. They left without me." She heard a sharp crack come from the shrubbery next to the building and whirled around.

It was only a squirrel. She turned her attention back to her conversation with Brenna. Good grief, she had to calm down and not jump at every little thing.

But, being honest with herself, Megan was terrified. She'd been involved with GDT for years—volunteering with their youth group, going on various corporate-sponsored internships—and now working this plum job for Zooby News. She couldn't afford to screw this up. And yet. That was the reasoning that had led her into a lot of bad decisions lately.

She thought of her father in his wheelchair, how often she dreamed of earning enough to send him to a state-of-the-art rehab center where he could regain the use of his legs. She'd read about such places, but they were miles away from this backwater and far beyond their family's budget, even with GDT's financial help.

She hoped that if she proved herself to be a real asset to GDT, she could either land a reporting job in New York and put money aside for that expensive therapy—or that Mr. Dahl would offer to pay for it himself as a reward for her loyalty and hard work. Her dad deserved it—and Megan deserved success. That was what had propelled her to where she was now.

But last night changed everything. There was a lot that she hadn't wanted to know—a lot of times when she looked the other way, like with what happened to Professor Davenport. Megan claimed she had an inquiring mind, but when it came to the way GDT protected its corporate image and assets, ignorance was bliss. She hoped Davenport and his family were all right, and suddenly realized that she *had* to find out whether they were or not.

Now Jeremiah—and apparently Claire—had disappeared—and Megan had seen with her own eyes the rough treatment Jeremiah got last night. No, the time had come for Megan to stand up and do what was right. She could see that now.

"They wouldn't tell me," she answered Brenna's question, knowing that she sounded whiny. "They just . . ."

The bushes crackled again.

Some squirrel's really having a party. That was Megan's last thought before a blow to the head knocked her unconscious.

TE: 12 DECEMBER 1998   EVIDENCE FILE #: 3.11.28.11

SC.: JOURNAL ENTRY

TES:

FROM THE JOURNAL OF JEREMIAH WHITNEY ON THE DAY OF HIS BAPTISM.

December 12, 1998

I got baptized today. Mom gave me this journal so I could write the story of my life. That feels like a really good idea, so I am going to do it every day if I can. That's my first goal as a member of the Church. After Dad baptized me he confirmed me a member and gave me the Holy Ghost, which I think I need.

Dad gave me a present today, too. Double presents because my birthday was Tuesday! But it's not a toy it's leather scriptures with my name on the in gold. Cool!! I think Dad is proud of me today. That feels good. I know I make him crazy with all my questions and weird ideas and stuff.

But I got baptized today!!!!!, It feels good.

CHAPTER TWENTY

Birthright

Jeremiah's nose was cold. He opened his eyes and looked around. He wasn't in his dorm room. Where was he? He sat up on his elbows and shifted his legs, which were encased in a . . . sleeping bag?

Camping. He hadn't been camping since High Adventure two summers ago. Why was he camping in the cold? He rubbed his eyes and face, wincing when he touched his cheek. He looked around. Lying several feet away, also in a sleeping bag, was Claire, her long, wavy hair mussed and tangled with pine needles. At the sight of her sweet face, so peaceful in sleep, everything came rushing back.

Claire was alive! And they were both free. It was a miracle, literally. How had it happened? How had they gotten away from Magus and that horrible, dingy basement?

• • •

"I'm worried about Jeremiah," Lilah mused out loud as they sped down the freeway. "I've been thinking about the DNA test results."

Porter cleared his throat warningly, and Lilah glanced at him. *Right. The two junior spies in the backseat.*

Sure enough, Simon piped up right away. "A DNA test? Because he was adopted?"

Porter shifted in his seat and glared at Simon. "Who said he was adopted?"

Simon started to answer, then stopped, looking at Brian. Porter looked back and forth between the two of them, wondering how much they knew. He remembered the listening device Simon had brought in that morning.

Brian. The little nosy parker. Porter would wring his neck unless he gave up some answers, soon.

Brian seemed to sense the threat. "Jeremiah told us, because he wanted me to help him investigate. I have connections," Brian confessed, without quite meeting Porter's eyes. Porter accepted the lie for the moment and turned back around.

• • •

Brenna's phone gave three beeps, then nothing more. "Megan? Megan!"

The call must have dropped. Or had someone interfered somehow? Fuming, Brenna replayed in her mind the conversation she had just had with Megan.

"They left you?" Brenna had asked incredulously. Megan was off her game once again. So much potential, but the girl was slipping up dangerously. "I thought you said they were your friends, Megan. Real friends don't do that."

She didn't want to come down too hard; she knew Megan was in a risky spot, commitment-wise. "Why'd they say that Jeremiah didn't come home last night?"

"They wouldn't say. I think they're suspicious."

"Suspicious? Then you're not doing your job. *Think.*" Brenna forced the menace out of her tone. "What did they say that could clue us in?"

"Lilah said something about Claire," Megan said.

Brenna furrowed her brow. That was news. "The perky girl with a crush on Jeremiah?"

"She left FHE and never came back. You wouldn't know anything about that, would you?"

Brenna had *not* liked the attitude she was getting from her protégée. "I hope you're not suggesting I do." She closed her eyes and rubbed her sore back. She knew part of her irritability had to do with the fact that the baby was sitting on her bladder right now. She stood up and bent over, willing the child to move.

"Listen, Megan," she had said as she stretched. "We're trying to keep him safe. Now, where did they go?"

"They wouldn't say," Megan had insisted. "They just . . ." And that's when the call had dropped.

Brenna's phone rang again. Megan. But no—when she checked her caller ID, she got a nasty surprise. Z was calling her. She did not need this right now. She took a deep breath and answered the call. "This is Brenna."

"Magus and his team have searched the building and environs. Jeremiah and the girl are gone. We're convinced that their disappearance is a sign that he's ready to receive the box. What did your agent find out from Jeremiah's friends?"

Brenna mentally cursed Megan for not giving her better information. "Nothing . . . yet. They left before she could find out their destination."

"You're kidding." His voice took on an edge. "We need to teleconference. Now. Get to the control room. I'll reach you there."

Brenna clicked off her phone. This wasn't going to be pleasant. Rubbing her belly protectively, she left her office.

• • •

Jeremiah heard a sharp crack in the brush behind him. He turned to see Ammon stepping into the clearing, carrying some dead branches. He smiled in a fatherly way. "Are you okay?"

Jeremiah stretched his neck and opened his eyes wide. Except for the bruises on his face where Magus had hit him, he felt fine—better than he had in days, actually.

"Yeah, I think so." He looked toward Claire's sleeping form. "Is she?"

Ammon smiled and nodded.

"So, why aren't we dead?" Jeremiah still couldn't believe it. He couldn't remember waking up so happy just to be alive—certainly not in the last several weeks. He felt like he was finally waking up from a nightmare that had begun on his fake birthday. Yes, his parents were still dead, and danger lurked everywhere. But Jeremiah felt—different.

Ammon asked, "Would you have died to protect this sacred trust?"

Jeremiah thought back to the night before—the peace that had come over him when he realized that Magus's threats were totally ineffective. That was when everything in Jeremiah's outlook had changed with a single burst of clarity. He had seen his promise to protect the box against an eternal backdrop, instead of with the myopic urgency of the moment. Threats didn't matter; obedience did. He nodded. "I thought we were going to die."

"The Lord has said that we must be tested like Abraham."

"Abraham?" Jeremiah asked, knowing that another one of Ammon's scripture stories was on the way. He didn't mind; Ammon had a way of making those old tales come alive. Jeremiah knew they were real—but they'd never felt as immediate as when Ammon talked about them. It was almost like Ammon had actually seen those things happen.

"The Lord commanded Abraham to kill his son, Isaac, as a sacrifice. Can you imagine what that must have been like? Because of his faith, Abraham agreed. But when he was ready to kill his only son, an angel appeared and stopped him. The angel pointed to a ram caught in the bushes, and Abraham sacrificed it instead of his son. We must be tested in the same way. Last night you were tested. You passed."

Jeremiah saw the power of that, but felt a little contrary. Last night had been the most harrowing experience of his life. Had that really been necessary—to put not only him, but poor, innocent Claire into extreme danger?

"So the Lord requires us to make sacrifices for no logical reason. And then when we make the sacrifice, He doesn't want it? I just don't get it."

Ammon gave him a look that was both gentle and challenging. "What did you learn about yourself last night?" He waited for a moment, looking at Jeremiah, then got up and walked over to a fire pit.

Jeremiah heard a rustle; Claire was starting to wake up. She struggled as if fighting someone in a dream. Jeremiah threw off his sleeping bag and rushed to her side. He took her by the shoulders and held her. "Claire! It's okay!"

She stared at him for a moment as if he were a stranger.

"Claire—look at me. It's Jeremiah. You're okay." Her eyes widened in recognition and she relaxed.

• • •

"Brenna!"

She jumped a little. She'd gotten to the security control room seconds before. It was deserted, dark, and cold, with the only light coming from the array of sophisticated monitors on the wall behind her. She hadn't expected company—not in person. She hated it when people sneaked up on her. Z did it often. He seemed to think it gave him an advantage.

Hand on her heart, she turned, peering at her boss, who stood in the deep shadows near the doorway. "You scared me. I thought this was supposed to be a teleconference."

He sauntered forward. "If you think we'd handle anything this important over the phone, then you don't know who this young man is. But if we can get him now, we can turn him." Z smiled sardonically, stopping a little too close to Brenna. He turned his attention to several tools laid out on the counter and idly began rolling an awl back and forth.

Brenna was unsure how to take this. She opted for aloofness. "Well, I haven't been briefed on the specifics, but I know how important he is. I have my agent checking his whereabouts right now."

"Really? Right now? His whereabouts?" Z had the awl in his hand now, tracing the lines in his palm with its sharp edge. He seemed fascinated by what he was doing.

Brenna nodded, hoping that Megan actually was where she said she was. She found herself getting more nervous by the second, both for herself and for her baby.

"No need," Z said, looking up at Brenna and grinning. "We already know where he is."

He pointed to the floor on the other side of the big, multiscreened telecommunications hub. Brenna squinted in the dim light and got a nasty shock. Megan sat on the floor underneath the long counter, securely bound and gagged. Brenna hadn't even noticed her when she'd walked in.

"She didn't miss her friends," Z said. "She let them go, and then lied about it. What else isn't she telling the truth about?" He looked down at Megan, who was shaking her head with wide, terrified eyes. He let out a little laugh. "Maybe her father needs to have another accident."

•   •   •

Lilah drove in silence, having turned off the radio after Porter had compulsively fiddled with it for several minutes. Silence was golden. But then Porter's phone squeaked; he'd gotten a text.

"What does it say?" asked Lilah.

"Mile Marker 3."

• • •

Claire and Jeremiah finished the huge breakfast Ammon had prepared for them over the fire: eggs basted in butter, and the thickest bacon Jeremiah had ever seen. It was delicious, and not just because Jeremiah realized he hadn't eaten dinner the night before. Claire started cleaning up their mess, but Ammon took her plate from her.

"I can do this," he assured her. "You have friends arriving soon. You must meet them." He set the dishes down for the moment and took Claire over to where the horses were tied. "Mahonri Moriancumer will take you."

Jeremiah followed them. "Mahonri Moriancumer?" That was laying on the gospel allusions a bit thick. "Are you kidding?"

Ammon shook his head, laughter in his piercing blue eyes. "But she goes by 'Bessie.'"

Unbelievable. Jeremiah rolled his eyes, and Ammon grinned.

"Actually, Ammon, before she goes, can I just talk to Claire for a second?"

Ammon nodded and walked back over to the breakfast

mess. Jeremiah took a step closer to Claire. Suddenly, gratitude overwhelmed him. This girl was amazing. Her bravery and unquestioning acceptance in the basement the night before—it blew him away. She was like Joan of Arc, or something. She looked up at him, waiting for him to speak.

"Claire, I'm sorry I couldn't tell him about the box. But I made a promise, and I couldn't break it. No matter what." He hoped she'd accept his apology. She had been kind and attentive all during breakfast, laughing at Ammon's jokes and eating with gusto. But he couldn't forget the fact that she had witnessed his awful, albeit necessary, action in the cave. She had seen it completely out of context—how could she possibly understand? How was there any way that she could forgive him and ever want to be around him again? Jeremiah didn't know, but he prayed that she would find a way.

She smiled, and he could tell that she miraculously didn't hold anything against him. "I don't know what happened last night. I don't know what I saw, but . . ." she faltered.

Jeremiah nodded, willing her to go on.

"This makes no sense, but I know you made the right choice."

Relief made Jeremiah's knees weak, and he stayed upright through sheer force of will. The love in Claire's eyes sent a thrill through Jeremiah, but even better was the feeling of relief at being understood and forgiven. He wanted to take her in his arms and . . . but then he remembered that

Ammon was standing five feet away. He dropped his eyes, embarrassed—and the moment was over.

Ammon came over and helped Claire onto Bessie's back.

"It's time," he said. "Claire, you must tell no one about this. Bessie knows the way. Jeremiah will join you soon." He slapped the mare's haunch. "All right, Bessie. Git!" The horse rode away with Claire on its back. Jeremiah watched them go, regretting with every atom in his body that he hadn't kissed Claire before she left.

• • •

Brian watched Porter carefully. He stood with his arms around Lilah, and Brian felt a rush of envy at their close, easy relationship. He dismissed the distracting thought and focused. He wanted to get photos of those DNA documents, but he had to do it without his beefy, quick-to-anger next-door neighbor catching him. That would be death. This operation required stealth tactics of the highest order. Fortunately, Brian was up to the task.

Lilah had parked her car just off the road near the mile marker, but Porter told them that he had no idea what they should do now, just that he felt like they should wait—for the moment, anyway.

So wait they did. Lilah wasn't keeping a close eye on her purse, where she had put the envelope with the DNA test results. It was just a matter of sliding them out the moment there was a distraction. Fortunately, his roommate excelled

at distracting her—and Simon didn't even realize how helpful he was.

"Declare your allegiance!" Simon yelled, brandishing a
long stick pulled from the brush. He squinted appreciatively
at the wilderness all around them. "Wouldn't this be a great
place for an orc invasion?"

"Oh, yeah," Lilah said. "And Porter could be a Tree
Man . . . Thing."

Brian stepped to the rear of the car where the others
couldn't see him. With his cell phone, he quickly took several photos of the DNA certificates.

"That's a good idea!" he heard Simon say. "You could
come crashing through the forest with all the other tree war-
riors."

As if on Simon's cue, the brush behind them snapped
sharply. Brian froze and noticed that the others had done the
same.

Claire appeared, riding out of the dense trees on horse-
back. As if she were the rodeo queen in a parade, she waved
at them all while reining in the horse with her other hand.
She dismounted and tied the horse to a tree. She hurried over
to the group. Lilah hugged her fiercely.

"Claire, what are you doing here?" asked Simon. He
looked delighted, as if this were all a show staged for his
benefit.

"It's a long story," Claire answered—meaning she didn't
want to talk about it.

"Where's Jeremiah?" asked Porter, his voice tense.

"He's safe." Tears welled up in Claire's eyes as she

looked at each of them in turn. "He's coming back, and he's going to need each of you."

Lilah gave Claire a careful looking-over and squeezed her tightly again. Claire hugged her back, burying her face in her friend's shoulder. *Perfect.* Brian carefully slid the envelope back into Lilah's purse.

Porter clearly wasn't happy with Claire's cryptic response. "What's 'safe' supposed to mean?"

Claire looked at him. It was as if she had matured overnight, somehow. The wide-eyed girl was gone, replaced by a sadder, wiser, yet more poised woman. She'd gone from pretty to beautiful in the space of a few hours.

"I'm not sure," she said. "I just know everything's going to be different."

• • •

A voice came from the telecom bank, automatically disguised as it passed through the cryptography software. "Have you located Jeremiah and the old man? We need him with the box. There hasn't been one of these out in the open since May 1888—that's 121 years. We can't risk losing its contents."

Z sighed, frustrated. He was so close to having all the information crucial to retrieving the box. This would be the coup that pushed him ahead of his rivals. He hated being interrupted—but he knew why the big boss was anxious. "The satellite hasn't located their exact position due to tree coverage, but we're certain they are in Manti."

"Send an agent immediately."

"Someone's already been dispatched. He'll intercept the exchange and bring the box and Jeremiah to you."

• • •

Ammon walked behind a tree, moved some heavy-looking branches, and picked up a canvas bag hidden underneath. Jeremiah looked at it; he knew that shape and what it meant. After all he had been through, he still wasn't sure how he felt about being entrusted with the box. It was connected to so much grief and pain in Jeremiah's mind; the two worst hours of his life had been spent in its presence. What could taking on the responsibility of it again mean for his future? He dreaded it, but he knew that he had already made his choice. He would take the box and face whatever happened next.

Ammon beckoned him over to sit with him on the fallen log near the fire, where they'd eaten breakfast together. "This is yours," Ammon said, nodding at the sack sitting in his lap.

Jeremiah nodded. "I know." He stared at it for a moment, then looked up into Ammon's eyes. "Can I ask you a question? Why couldn't that guy in the cave touch the box, but I could?"

"The box can only be handled by those who are called to do so. You have been called and have proven yourself; therefore, only you can touch the box and use its contents."

Its contents. *Of course.* In all Jeremiah's pondering

about the box and how he had lost it, he hadn't spared much thought for what was *inside* it. So he was to be more than a simple steward? He had imagined that he would merely be its caretaker, eventually passing it onto someone else when he got old like Ammon.

This sacred trust, as the woman at the library had called it—it suddenly seemed much broader in scope—and more dangerous. Jeremiah swallowed.

Ammon smiled faintly as if he could read Jeremiah's thoughts, then grew earnest again. "No matter your worthiness, you are free to choose how it will be used—for good or ill. That makes you a target for many."

Even more of a target than I already have been. But his musing was tinged with acceptance, not bitterness.

"Do you still want it?" Ammon asked.

Jeremiah realized that he did. After last night—and after Ammon's confirmation this morning that he'd passed a crucial test—Jeremiah knew that he did want the responsibility. His parents had died in order for him to have it; he realized that. He wanted to honor their sacrifice and do whatever was required of him. He nodded firmly.

"Have you decided what you learned about yourself last night?" Ammon asked.

Jeremiah remembered his flash of insight of the night before. Earthly threats mattered very little anymore. He would do what he had been called to do.

"That the Lord can trust me."

Ammon slowly handed him the bag. Jeremiah took it

into his arms carefully and felt the weight of grave responsibility sink down upon his shoulders.

"Jeremiah, you have a great work to do." Once again, Ammon seemed to know what Jeremiah was feeling. "But you won't be alone. You have friends. You have me." The old man paused, and in that moment Jeremiah realized that Ammon had a deep, grandfatherly affection for him. "But most of all, you have God. He'll shape your back to bear the burden placed upon it. Call on Him often." Ammon waited, and Jeremiah felt the words sink into his heart. "It's time to go," Ammon said. He and Jeremiah stood and went to the horses.

• • •

Magus sped down the freeway on his bullet bike. He was shocked and relieved that Z had given him the chance to make up for his catastrophic mistake by sending him after Jeremiah today. He wouldn't wait to give Jeremiah the chance to use supernatural powers to escape this time. This time, he'd strike first. Jeremiah and the box would be his by the end of the day, and he would be handsomely rewarded when he brought his quarry back to his superiors. He'd do this right; he was ready.

• • •

Ammon and Jeremiah rode high into the hills, but they seemed to be going a different direction than they had the night that Ammon took him to the cave. They entered a clearing, and in the valley below them stood the Manti temple, gleaming in the winter sunlight.

Ammon reined in his horse and waited for Jeremiah to follow suit. "Go ahead, ask. You have a right."

Jeremiah looked at him. How was Ammon reading his mind? It was probably a spiritual gift, but it felt a little spooky. He guessed it didn't matter, and decided to voice his question.

"You knew my father," he said.

"Knew? I *know* your father," Ammon answered.

Jeremiah nearly fell off his horse in shock. His father was *alive?* Then why hadn't he stayed with Jeremiah's mother—why had they given him up for adoption? Had they gotten divorced, or had their relationship been illicit? Questions raged like a storm through his heart. He trusted Ammon, though, so he kept quiet and waited for him to tell his story.

"Shortly after His resurrection, Jesus visited the Nephites in the Americas. He called twelve disciples. Before He left, He asked each of them what they desired the most. Three said they wanted to remain on earth, serving others until His Second Coming. He granted them their desire."

"The Three Nephites," Jeremiah said, still waiting for his answer.

Ammon smiled slightly. "One of them is your father."

Jeremiah's jaw dropped, and his eyes filled with tears. That was impossible.

Wasn't it? No, of course not. But the implications staggered him.

He realized once again that his testimony wasn't as robust as it should be. In his mind, he went back to basics, the way his mother had always taught him to do when he had a serious doubt about the gospel. Start with truth and go forward, as if building a geometric proof. He knew the Book of Mormon was true—absolutely. Therefore, the Three Nephites were real—living among mortals in a unique, immortal state of some kind until the Savior's Second Coming.

He hadn't ever really stopped to imagine what their long lives might entail, but his first thought would have been that they went around together, like some longstanding missionary companionship—except that there were three of them. But that actually sounded pretty awful—living with just two other guys for two thousand years, even if they did roam around like superheroes—saving people, warning folks in danger, healing the sick. So—what happened when immortals had children?

"What—what does that make me?" he wondered aloud.

Ammon clapped him on the shoulder. "Take some time. Ponder and prepare. I'll see you on the road."

He turned his horse and rode away. Jeremiah looked across the clearing; he was at the edge of a cliff. All of Manti spread out before him, the white temple with its twin silver cupolas rising up from the hill, front and center.

He went over Ammon's disclosure again. His father was one of the Three Nephites? He hadn't ever thought that people like that would have families—but why wouldn't they?

Was his mother still alive as well? And how did Ammon

know his parents? What was his role in all that had happened when Jeremiah had been adopted? And what did any of this have to do with the box that was now back in Jeremiah's care? The one answer Ammon had given him raised another hundred questions.

Jeremiah stared out at the temple's gleaming walls and tried to make sense of everything he had learned and endured. Again, he thought of his mother's advice: go back to basics. Just as the temple stood alone in a confusing world, Jeremiah saw certain core truths rising up from the midst of all his confusion. The Lord was mindful of him and had a specific mission planned for him. He had placed loyal friends in Jeremiah's life—Ammon, Porter, Claire—who would support him through anything.

So he had questions. Ammon had once told him that questions were more important than answers. If that was true, Jeremiah was well armed. For now, he would get by.

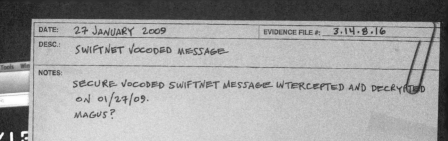

DATE: 27 JANUARY 2009   EVIDENCE FILE #: 3.14.8.16
DESC.: SWIFTNET VOCODED MESSAGE
NOTES: SECURE VOCODED SWIFTNET MESSAGE INTERCEPTED AND DECRYPTED
ON 01/27/09.
MAGUS?

SWIF

CURE TRANSMISSION

* * * * * *

: L. Dahl, GDT, Provo, Utah

om: M. Donovan, L3G10N Western States Cell

C: Gainsborough

----

ir, I have the quarry in my sights and have confirmed that he is
ow in possession of the box. I expect to apprehend both and take
hem west to the Juab safe house within the hour. I'll report back
o you in full detail when I get there. I thank you for placing
our trust in me after the events of last night. I am better
prepared for this encounter, and I give you my solemn oath that
you will not be disappointed again. This is Magus, over and out.